John Earle

The Deeds of Beowulf

John Earle

The Deeds of Beowulf

ISBN/EAN: 9783337366575

Printed in Europe, USA, Canada, Australia, Japan

Cover: Foto ©Andreas Hilbeck / pixelio.de

More available books at **www.hansebooks.com**

THE DEEDS OF BEOWULF

AN ENGLISH EPIC OF THE EIGHTH CENTURY DONE INTO MODERN PROSE

By JOHN EARLE

OXFORD
AT THE CLARENDON PRESS
1892

THE DEEDS OF BEOWULF

THE FIRST PART.

Prologue. The chivalry of the Danish Empire. The coming of Scyld and his glorious career. The birth of Beaw and the exemplary pursuits of his youth. The passing of Scyld.

WHAT ho! we have heard tell of the grandeur of the imperial kings of the spear-bearing Danes in former days, how those ethelings promoted bravery. Often did Scyld of the Sheaf wrest from harrying bands, from many tribes, their convivial seats; the dread of him fell upon warriors, whereas he had at the first been a lonely foundling;––of all that (humiliation) he lived to experience solace; he waxed great under the welkin, he flourished with trophies, till that every one of the neighbouring peoples over the sea were constrained to obey 10 him, and pay trewage:––that was a good king!

To him was born a son to come after him, a young (prince) in the palace, whom God sent for the people's comfort. He (God) knew the hard calamity, what they had erst endured when they were without a king for a long while; and in consideration thereof

B

the Lord of Life, the Ruler of Glory accorded to them a time of prosperity.

Beowulf (i. e. Beaw) was renowned, his fame sprang
20 wide; heir of Scyld in the Scedelands. So ought a young chief to work with his wealth, with gracious largesses, while in his father's nurture; that in his riper age willing comrades may in return stand by him at the coming of war, and that men may do his bidding. Eminence must, in every nation, be attained by deeds (worthy) of PRAISE.

As for Scyld, he departed, at the destined hour, full of exploit, to go into the Master's keeping. They then carried him forth to the shore of the sea, his faithful
30 comrades, as he himself had requested, while he with his words held sway as lord of the Scyldings; dear chief of the land, he had long tenure of power.

There at hythe stood the ship with ringèd prow, glistening fresh, and outward bound; convoy for a prince. Down laid they there the lovèd chief, dispenser of jewels, on the lap of the ship, the illustrious (dead) by the mast. There was store of precious things, ornaments from remote parts, brought together; never heard I of craft comelier fitted with slaughter weapons
40 and campaigning harness, with bills and breast-mail :— in his keeping lay a multitude of treasures, which were to pass with him far away into the watery realm. Not at all with less gifts, less stately opulence, did they outfit him, than those had done, who at the first had sent him forth, lone over the wave, when he was an infant. Furthermore they set up by him a gold-wrought banner, high over his head; they let the

holm bear him, gave him over to ocean; sad was
their soul, mourning their mood.   Men do not know 50
to say of a sooth, not heads of Halls, men of mark
under heaven, Who received that burthen!

I.

**King Hrothgar, his popularity.   The building of Heorot,
and the happy life of the Court.   Grendel.**

Then was in the towers Beowulf of the Scyldings,
the dear king of his people, for a long time famous
among the nations—his father was gone otherwhere,
patriarch from family seat—till in succession to him ·
was born the lofty Healfdene; he governed while
he lived, old and warlike, contented Scyldings.   To
him four children, one after another, awoke in the 60
world: Heorogar commander of armies and Hrothgar
and Halga the good: I heard that Elan queen [of
Ongentheow] was consort of the warlike Scylfing.

To Hrothgar was given martial spirit, warlike ambi-
tion; insomuch that his cousins gladly took him for
leader, until the young generation grew up, a mighty
regiment of clansmen.   Into his mind it came, that he
would give orders for men to construct a hall-building,
a great mead-house, (greater) than the children of men 70
had ever heard tell of; and that therewithin he would
freely deal out to young and old what God should give
him, save people's land and lives of men.

Then I heard of work widely proclaimed to many
a tribe throughout this world, to make a fair gathering-
place of people.   His plan was in good time accomplished, with a quickness surprizing to men; so that
it was all ready, the greatest of hall-buildings.   He

gave it the name of Heorot, he who with his word had
80 wide dominion.   He belied not his announcement;—
rings he distributed, treasure at the banquet.   The hall
towered aloft, high and with pinnacles spanning the
air; awaited the scathing blasts of destructive flame.
No appearance was there as yet of knife-hatred starting
up between son-in-law and father-in-law in revenge of
blood.

Then the outcast creature, he who dwelt in darkness,
with torture for a time endured that he heard joyance day by day, loud sounding in hall; there was
90 the swough of the harp, the ringing song of the
minstrel.

Said one who was skilled to narrate from remote
time the primæval condition of men; quoth he—
"The Almighty made the earth, the country radiant
"with beauty, all that water surroundeth, delighting in
"magnificence.   He ordained Sun and Moon, lumi-
"naries for light to the dwellers on earth, and adorned
"the rustic regions with branches and leaves; life also
"he created for all the kinds that live and move."

100   Thus they, the warrior-band, in joyance lived and
full delight;—until that one began to work atrocity, a
fiend in the hall.   The grim visitant was called
Grendel, the dread mark-ranger, he who haunted
moors, fen and fastness: — the unblessed man
had long time kept the abode of monsters, ever
since the Creator had proscribed them.   On Cain's
posterity did the eternal Lord wreak that slaughter,
for that he slew Abel.   He profited not by that
110 violence; but He banished him far away, the Maker
for that crime banished him from mankind.   From

that origin all strange broods awoke, eotens and elves and ogres, as well as giants who warred against God long time ;—He repaid them due retribution.

II.

Grendel, his successful raid.   The dejection of Hrothgar and his court.

He set out then as soon as night was come, to explore the lofty house ; how the mailèd Danes had after carousal bestowed themselves in it.   So he found therein a princely troop sleeping after feast ;   they knew not sorrow, desolation of men.   The baleful wight, grim and 120 greedy, was ready straight, fierce and furious, and in their sleep he seized thirty of the thanes ; thence hied him back, yelling over his prey, to go to his home with the war-spoils, and reach his habitation.   Then was in the dawning and with early day the war-craft of Grendel plain to the grooms ; then was upraised after festivity the voice of weeping, a great cry in the morning.   The illustrious ruler, the honoured 130 prince, sät wobegone ; majestic rage he tholed, he endured sorrow for his thanes :—since they had surveyed the track of the monster, of the accursed goblin ;—that contest was too severe, horrible, and prolonged.   It was not a longer space, but the interval of one night, that he again perpetrated a huger carnage ; and he recked not of it—outrage and atrocity ; he was too fixed in those things.   Then was it not hard to find some who sought a resting-place elsewhere more at large, a bed among the castle-bowers, when to 140 them was manifested and plainly declared by conspicuous proof the malice of the hell-thane ;—whoever had once

escaped the fiend did from thenceforward hold himself farther aloof and closer. So domineered and nefariously warred he single against them all, until that the best of houses stood empty. The time was long; twelve winters' space did the Friend of the Scyldings suffer indignity, woes of every kind, unbounded sorrows;
150 and so in process of time it became openly known to the sons of men through ballads in lamentable wise, that Grendel warred continually against Hrothgar; he waged malignant hostilities, violence and feud, many seasons, unremitting strife; he would not have peace with any man of the Danish power, or remove the life-bale, or compound for tribute; nor could any of the senators expect worthy compensation at the hands of
160 the destroyer; the foul ruffian, a dark shadow of death, was pursuing the venerable and the youthful alike. He prowled about and lay in wait; at nights he continually held the misty moors;—men do not know in what direction hell's agents move in their rounds.

Many were the atrocities which the foe of mankind, the grisly prowler, oft accomplished, hard indignities,—Heorot he occupied, the richly decorated hall, in dark nights—yet was he by no means able to come nigh the throne, sacred to God, nor did he share the sentiment thereof.
170 That was a huge affliction for the friend of the Scyldings, heart breaking. Many a time and oft did the realm sit in conclave; they meditated on a remedy, what course it were best for them, soul-burthened men, to take against these awful horrors. Sometimes they vowed at idol fanes, honours of sacrifice; with words they prayed that the Goblin-queller would afford them

relief against huge oppressions. Such was their custom, heathens' religion ; they thought of hell in 180 their imagination ; they were not aware of the Maker, the Judge of actions, they knew not God the Governor, nor did they at all understand how to glorify the Crowned Head of the heavens, the Ruler of glory.

It is woe for him who is impelled by headlong per- versity to plunge his soul into the gulph of fire ; not to believe in consolation nor in any way turn :—well is it for him who is permitted, after death-day, to visit the Lord, and claim sanctuary in the Father's arms.

III.

The voyage of the hero. A parley.

Thus was the son of Healfdene perpetually tossed with the trouble of that time; the sapient man was 190 unable to avert the woe. Too heavy, horrible, and protracted was the struggle which had overtaken that people ; tribulation cruel, hugest of nocturnal pests.

That in his distant home learnt a thane of Hygelac's, a brave man among the Goths ; he learnt the deeds of Grendel; he was of mankind strongest in might in the day of this life ; he was of noble birth and of robust growth. He ordered a wave-traveller, a good one, to be prepared for him ; said he would pass over the swan- 200 road and visit the gallant king, the illustrious ruler, inasmuch as he was in need of men. That adventure was little grudged him by sagacious men, though he was dear to them ; they egged on the dareful spirit, they observed auguries. The brave man had selected champions of the Leeds of the Goths, the keenest whom he could find ; with fourteen in company he took

to ship ;— a swain for pilot, a water-skilled man, pointed
out the landmarks.

210   Time went on ; the floater was on the waves, the
boat under the cliff.   Warriors ready dight mounted
on the prow ; currents eddied, surf against the beach ;
lads bore into the ship's lap bright apparel, gallant
harness of war ; the men, the brave men on adventure,
shoved off the tight-timbered craft.   So the foamy-
necked floater went forth over the swelling ocean
urged by the wind, most like to a bird ; till that in
220 due time, on the next day, the coily-stemmed cruiser
had made such way that the voyagers saw land, sea-cliffs
gleaming, hills towering, headlands stretching out to
sea ; then was the voyage accomplished, the water-
passage ended.   Then lightly up the Weder Leeds
and sprang ashore, they made fast the sea-wood, they
shook out their sarks, their war-weeds, they thanked
God for that their seafaring had been easy.

230   Then from his rampart did the Scyldings' warden, he
who had to guard the sea-cliffs, espy men bearing over
bulwark bright shields, accoutrements ready for action ;
—curiosity urged him with impassioned thoughts (to
learn) who those men were.   Off he set then to the shore,
riding on horseback, thane of Hrothgar ; powerfully he
brandished a huge lance in his hands, and he demanded
with authoritative words—"Who are ye arm-bearing
"men, fenced with mail-coats, who have come thus with
240 "proud ship over the watery high-way, hither over the
"billows?   Long time have I been in fort, stationed on
"the extremity of the country ; I have kept the coast-
"guard, that on the land of the Danes no enemy with
"ship-harrying might be able to do hurt :—never have

"shield-bearing men 'more openly attempted to land
"here; nor do ye know beforehand the pass-word of
"our warriors, the confidential token of kinsmen.
"I never saw, of eorlas upon ground, a finer figure
"in harness than is one of yourselves; he is no mere
"goodman bedizened with armour, unless his look 250
"belies him, his unique aspect. Now I am bound to
"know your nationality, before ye on your way hence
"as explorers at large proceed any further into the land
"of the Danes. Now ye foreigners, mariners of the
"sea, ye hear my plain meaning; haste is best to let me
"know whence your comings are."

IV.

**Beowulf explains their visit to the Warden's satisfaction.
Thereupon he guides their march to Heorot. The
Warden returns.**

To him the chiefest gave answer; the captain of the
band unlocked the treasure of words: "We are people
"of Gothic race, and hearth-fellow of Hygelac. My 260
"father was celebrated among the nations, a noble
"commander by the name of Ecgtheow; he lived to
"see many years, ere he departed an aged man out
"of his mansion; he is quickly remembered by every
"worshipful man all over the world. We with
"friendly intent have come to visit thy lord, the son
"of Healfdene, the guardian of his people; be thou
"good to us with instructions! We have for the
"illustrious prince of the Danes a great message; there 270
"is no need to be dark about the matter, as I suppose.
"Thou knowest if it is so as we have heard say for a

"truth, that among the Scyldings some strange depre-
"dator, a mysterious author of deeds, in the darkness
"of night inflicts in horrible wise monstrous atrocity,
"indignity, and havoc.   Of this I can, in all sincerity
"of heart, teach Hrothgar a remedy; how he, so wise
280 "and good, shall overpower the enemy; if for him
"the fight of afflictions was ever destined to take a
"turn, better times to come again, and the seethings
"of anguish grow calmer; or else for ever here-
"after tholeth he a time of tribulation, sore distress, so
"long as the best of houses resteth there upon her
"eminence."

The Warden addressed them, where he sat on his
horse, an officer undaunted: "Of every particular
"must a sharp esquire know the certainty as to words
"and works—any one who hath a sense of duty.   I
290 "gather from what I hear that this is a friendly band
"to the lord of the Scyldings.   March ye forward
"bearing weapons and weeds, I will guide you: likewise
"I will command my kinsmen thanes honourably to
"keep against every foe your vessel, the newly dight,
"the boat on the beach: until the neck-laced craft shall
"bear back again over the water-streams her dear lord
"to Wedermark.   To such a benign adventurer is it
300 "given, that he passeth unscathed through the en-
"counter of battle."

They proceeded then on their march; the vessel
remained still, rode on her cable, the wide-bosomed
ship, at anchor fast;—the boar-figures shone, over the
cheek-guards, prankt with gold, ornate and hard-
welded;—the farrow kept guard.   In fighting mood
they raged along, the men pushed forward; down-hill

they ran together, until they could see the Hall
structure, gallant and gold-adorned; that was to
dwellers on earth the most celebrated of all mansions 310
under the sky, that in which the Ruler dwelt; the
gleam of it shot over many lands. Then did the
warrior point out to them the court of the valiant,
which was now conspicuous;—that they could go
straight to it. Like a man of war, he wheeled about
his horse, and spake a parting word; "It is time
"for me to go; may the allwielding Father graciously
"keep you safe in adventures! I will to the sea, to
"keep guard against hostile force."

V.

Arrival and accost. Beowulf sends in his name.

The street was stone-paven; the path guided the 320
banded men. The war-corslet shone, hard, hand-
locked; the polished ring-iron sang in its meshes, when
they in grim harness now came marching to the Hall.
The sea-weary men set down their broad shields,
bucklers mortal hard, against the terrace of that mansion.
Then they seated themselves on the bench;—their mail-
coats rang, harness of warriors;—the spears stood,
sea-men's artillery, stacked together, ash-timber with 330
tip of grey; the iron troop was accoutred worthily.
Then a proud officer there questioned the martial
crew as to their kindred:—"Whence bring ye
"damasked shields, gray sarks, and visored helms;—a
"pile of war shafts? I am Hrothgar's herald and
"esquire. Never saw I foreigners, so many men, loftier
"looking. I think that ye for daring, not at all of des-

"perate fortune, but for courageous emprize, have come
340 "to visit Hrothgar."

To him then with gallant bearing answered the proud
leed of the Wederas; words spake he back, firm
under helmet:—"We are Hygelac's table-fellows; my
"name is Beowulf. I will expound mine errand to the
"son of Healfdene, to the illustrious prince, to thy
"lord, if he will deign us that we may approach him
"so good."

Wulfgar addressed them—that was a leed of the
Wendlas; his courage had been witnessed by many, his
350 valour and wisdom:—"Thereanent will I ask the Friend
"of the Danes, the Scyldings' lord, the ring-dispenser,
"according as thou dost petition, the illustrious chief
"(will I ask) concerning thy visit; and to thee promptly
"declare the answer, which the brave prince is pleased
"to give me."

Thereupon he returned briskly to where Hrothgar
sate, old and hoary, with his guard of warriors: he
went with gallant bearing till he took his stand before
the shoulders of the Danish prince; he knew the
360 custom of nobility. Wulfgar addressed himself to his
liege lord: "Here are arrived, come from far, over
"the circuit of ocean, men of the Goths; the com-
"panions name their chief Beowulf. They make peti-
"tion, that they, my prince, may be permitted to
"exchange discourse with thee: do not thou award
"them a refusal of thy conversation, benignant Hrothgar!
"They by their war-harness appear worthy of the rever-
"ence of eorlas; certainly the chief is a valiant man,
"he who has conducted those martial comrades
370 "hither."

VI

The old king knows all about him, and orders him to
be admitted. Beowulf explaineth his visit and enter-
prizeth the battle to fight the foe. He will remove
the scourge, or die in the attempt.

Hrothgar, crown of Scyldings, uttered speech;
"I knew him when he was a page. His good old
"father was Ecgtheow by name; to whose. home
"Hrethel of the Goths gave over his only daughter;
"it is his offspring surely, his grown-up son, that is
"hither come, come to visit a loyal friend. Sure
"enough they did say that—the sailors who carried
"thither for compliment the presents to the Goths—
"that he hath thirty men's strength in his handgrip, a 380
"valiant campaigner. Him hath holy God of high
"grace sent to us, sent to the western Danes, as
"I hope, against Grendel's terror; I must proffer the
"brave man treasures for his greatheartedness. Be
"thou full of alacrity, request the banded friends to
"enter, one and all, into my presence. Say to them
"moreover expressly with words, that they are welcome
"visitors to the Danish leeds." [Then to the door of
the hall Wulfgar went] he announced his message :— 390
"To you I am commanded to say by my chieftain the
"lord of the eastern Danes, that he knoweth your noble
"ancestry, and ye to him are, over the sea-waves, men
"of hardihood, welcome hither. Now ye can go, in
"your warlike equipage, with helm on head, to the
"presence of Hrothgar; leave the war-boards, here to
"abide, and the wooden battle-shafts till the parley is

"over." Up then arose the prince: about him many
400 a trooper, a splendid band of thanes; some remained
there, they kept the armour, as their brave captain
bade. They formed all together, as the officer (Wulfgar) showed the way, under the roof of Heorot; [he
went with courage high] with a firm look under his
helmet, till he took his stand in the royal chamber.
Beowulf uttered a speech—on him his byrnie shone,
a curious net-work linkéd by cunning device of the
artificer—" To Hrothgar hail ! I am Hygelac's kinsman
"and cousin-thane ; I have undertaken many exploits in
410 "youngsterhood. To me on my native soil the affair of
"Grendel became openly known; seafaring men say that
"this hall do stand, fabric superb, of every trooper empty
"and useless, as soon as the light of evening under the
"cope of heaven is hidden from view. Then did my
"people, the best of them, sagacious fellows, O royal
"Hrothgar, insense me that I should visit thee ; be-
"cause they knew the strength of my might ; they had
"themselves been spectators when I came off my cam-
420 "paign battered by foes, where I bound five monsters,
"humbled the eoten brood ; and in the waves I slew
"nickers in the night-time, I ran narrow risks, avenged
"the grievance of the Wederas—they had been ac-
"quainted with grief—a grinding I gave the spoilers ;—
"and now against Grendel I am bound, against that
"formidable one, single-handed, to champion the quar-
"rel against the giant. Wherefore I will now petition
"thee, prince of the glorious Danes, thou roof-tree of
"the Scyldings, one petition ; that thou refuse me
430 "not, oh thou shelter of warriors, thou imperial lord
"of nations, now I have come from such a distance,

"that I may have the task alone—I and my band of
"eorls, this knot of hardy men—to purge Heorot.
"I have learnt too that the terrible one out of bravado
"despises weapons; I therefore will forgo the same—
"as I hope that Hygelac my prince may be to me of
"mood benignant,—that I bear not sword or broad
"shield, or yellow buckler, to the contest; but with
"handgrip I undertake to encounter the enemy, and
"contend for life, foe to foe; there shall he whom 440
"death taketh resign himself to the doom of the Lord.

"I suppose that he will, if he can have his way, in
"the hall of battle devour fearlessly the men of the
"Goths, just as he often did the power of the Hreth-
"men. Thou wilt not need to cover my head (with
"a mound), but he will have me all blood-besprent, if
"death taketh me; he will bear away the gory corpse
"with intent to feast upon it, the solitary ranger will eat
"it remorselessly, will stain the moor-swamps; no need 450
"wilt thou have to care any longer for the disposal of
"my body. Send to Hygelac, if Hild take me, the
"matchless armour that protects my breast, bravest
"of jackets;—that is a relic of Hrethla's, a work
"of Wéland's. Wyrd goeth ever as she is bound."

VII.

**Hrothgar embraces his visitor's offer, and pours out
the tale of his misery. The new comers are feasted
in the hall.**

Hrothgar, crown of Scyldings, uttered speech:
"For pledgèd rescue thou, Beowulf my friend, and at
"honour's call, hast come to visit us. Thy father

460 "did fight out a mighty feud; he was the banesman of
"Heatholaf among the Wylfings; then the nation could
"not keep him for dread of invasion. Therefrom he
"went over the yeasty waves to visit the Southron folk
"of the Danes, of the honourable Scyldings, at the time
"when I had just then become king over the Danish
"folk, and in my prime swayed the jewel-stored
"treasure-city of heroes: when Heregar my elder
"brother was dead, no longer living, Halfdene's son.
470 "He was better than I! Afterwards I composed the
"feud for money; I sent to the Wylfings over the
"water's ridge ancient treasures; he swore oaths (of
"homage) to me.

    "It is a sorrow for me in my soul to tell to any mortal
"man what humiliation, what horrors, Grendel hath
"brought upon me in Heorot with his malignant strata-
"gems.   My hall-troop, my warrior band, is reduced to
"nothing; Wyrd hath swept them away in the hideous
"visitation of Grendel.   God unquestionably can arrest
480 "the fell destroyer in his doings.   Full oft they
"boasted when refreshed with beer, troop - fellows
"over the ale-can, that they in the beer-hall would
"receive Grendel's onset with clash of swords.   Then
"was this mead-hall at morning-tide, this royal saloon
"bespattered with gore, at blush of dawn, all the bench-
"timber was reeking with blood, the hall with deadly
"gore; so much the less owned I of trusty lieges, of
"dear nobility, when death had taken those away.
490   "Sit now to banquet, and merrily share the feast, brave
"captain, with (thy) fellows, as thy mind moves thee."

    Then was there for the Goth-men all together, in the
beer-hall, a table cleared; there the resolute men went

to sit in the pride of their strength. A thane attended
to the service; one who bore in his hand a decorated
ale-can; he poured forth the sheer nectar. At times
a minstrel sang, clear-voiced in Heorot; there was social
merriment, a brave company of Danes and Wederas.

VIII.

Unferth the king's orator is jealous. He baits the young
adventurer, and in a scoffing speech dares him to a
night-watch for Grendel. Beowulf is angered, and
thus he is drawn out to boast of his youthful feats.

Unferth made a speech, Ecglaf's son; he who sate 500
at the feet of the Scyldings' lord, broached a quarrel-
some theme—the adventure of Beowulf the high-souled
voyager was great despite to him, because he grudged
that any other man should ever in the world achieve
more exploits under heaven than he himself:—"Art
"thou that Beowulf, he who strove with Breca
"on open sea in swimming-match, where ye twain out
"of bravado explored the floods, and foolhardily in
"deep water jeoparded your lives? nor could any man, 510
"friend or foe, turn the pair of you from the dismal
"adventure! What time ye twain plied in swimming,
"where ye twain covered with your arms the awful
"stream, meted the sea-streets, buffeted with hands,
"shot over ocean; the deep boiled with waves, a
"wintry surge. Ye twain in the realm of waters
"toiled a se'nnight; he at swimming outvied thee, had
"greater force. Then in morning hour the swell cast
"him ashore on the Heathoram people, whence he 520
"made for his own patrimony, dear to his Leeds he
"made for the land of the Brondings, a fair strong-

D

"hold, where he was lord of folk, of city, and of rings.
"All his boast to thee-ward, Beanstan's son soothly
"fulfilled. Wherefore I anticipate for thee worse luck—
"though thou wert everywhere doughty in battle-shocks,
"in grim war-tug—if thou darest bide in Grendel's way
"a night-long space."

530   Beowulf son of Ecgtheow uttered speech :—" Lo,
"big things hast thou, my friend Unferth, beer-
"exalted, spoken about Breca; hast talked of his
"adventure! Rightly I claim, that I have proved
"more sea-power, more buffetings in waves, than any
"other man. He and I used to talk when we were
"pages, and we used to brag of this—we were both
"of us at that time in youngsterhood— how that we two
"would out on the main and put our lives in jeopardy;
"and that we matched so. Drawn sword we had,
540 "as we at swimming plied, firm in hand: we meant
"to guard us against the whale-fishes. Not a whit
"from me could he further fleet on sea-waves, swifter
"on holm; not from him would I. So we twain kept
"together in the sea for the space of five nights, till
"the flood parted us, the seething billows, coldest
"weather, darkening night, and a fierce wind from the
"north came dead against us; rough were the waves.
550 "The sea-fishes' temper was stirred; and then it was
"that my body-sark, firm, hand-locked, gave me help
"against the spiteful ones; the plaited war-jacket lay
"about my breast, gold-pranked. Me to bottom dragged
"a spotty monster, tight the grim thing had me in grip;
"nathless 'twas given me that I got at the vermin
"with point, with hand-bill; combat dispatched the
"mighty sea-brute by my hand.

IX.

Beowulf continues his story; and tells how he made
   havoc of the sea-monsters. He waxes warm, and
   flouts the orator. He vows to face Grendel.
Restoration of social harmony, whereof the queen
   is the centre. Hrothgar solemnly commits to
   Beowulf the night-ward of Heorot.

"As repeatedly as the spiteful assailants shrewdly 560
"pressed me, I served them (liberally) with precious
"sword as was meet. They did not have their slaugh-
"terous revel, the foul brigands, that they should eat
"me up sitting around their supper, by the floor of the
"sea; but (on the contrary) next morning, wounded with
"weapons along the wrack of the wave, they lay high
"and dry; by swords they had their quietus, so that
"never afterwards about the swelling highway should
"they let seafaring men of their destined course.

   "Light came from the East, the bright signal of God; 570
"the waves grew calm, so that I was able to see the
"forelands, the windy walls.   Fortune often rescues
"the warrior, if he is not fated to die; provided that his
"courage is sound! Anyhow 'twas my good luck, that
"I slew with the sword nine nicors. Never did I hear
"of a harder fight under heaven's roof in the night-
"time, nor of a man more distressed in ocean streams;
"howbeit I escaped the clutch of foes with my life,
"though worn and spent. Me the sea upcast, the 580
"swirling flood, upon the land of the Fins, the heaving
"billow. I never heard say aught by thee of such deadly
"fightings, sword-clashings: Breca never yet, at war

"play, not he nor you, deed achieved so valorously
"with flashing swords—of that I brag not much—
"though thou wast banesman to thy brother, thy next
"of kin ; for which thou shalt in hell damnation dree,
590 "though doughty be thy wit.   I say to thee of a sooth,
"thou son of Ecglaf, that never had Grendel the foul
"ruffian made such a tale of horrors for thy prince,
"such disgrace in Heorot, if thy courage were, if thy
"spirit were, so formidable as thou thyself claimest.
"But he hath found out that he need not greatly fear re-
"prisals, grisly edge-clash, from your people, the mighty
"Scyldings ; he taketh blackmail, respecteth no one of
"the people of the Danes, but maketh a sport of war,
600 "slaughtereth and feasteth :—no thought hath he of a
"fight with the spear-Danes.   But now shall the Goth
"show him erelong puissance and emprize in the way
"of war.   After that, he who can shall go proud into
"the mead-hall, when over the sons of men the morning
"light of another day, the sun, with radiance clothed,
"shall shine from the south."

Then was in bliss the dispenser of wealth, greyhaired and militant ; he believed in help ; the prince of
610 the glorious Danes, the shepherd of the people, perceived in Beowulf a resolute purpose.   There was
laughter of mighty men ; music sounded ; the words
(of song) were jovial.

Wealhtheow moved forward, Hrothgar's queen, mindful of ceremonies ; she greeted in her gold array the
men in Hall ; and then the noble lady presented the
beaker first to the sovereign of the east-Danes, wished
him blithe at the banquet, and dear to his Leeds ;—he
merrily enjoyed the feast and the Hall-cup, valiant king.

Then the Helming princess went the round, to elder 620
and to younger, every part; handed the jewelled cup;
till the moment came, that she, the diademed queen,
with dignity befitting, brought the mead-cup nigh to
Beowulf; she greeted the Leed of the Goths, she
thanked God with wise choice of words, for that her
desire was come to pass, that she in any warrior believed for remedy of woes. He, the death-doing warrior,
accepted the beaker at Wealhtheow's hand, and then he 630
descanted, elate for battle;—Beowulf son of Ecgtheow
uttered speech: "I undertook that, when I went on
"board, and sate on the sea-boat, with the company of
"my fellows, that I once for all would work out the will
"of your Leeds, or fall in the death-struggle, in the
"grip of the fiend. I am bound as an eorl to fulfil the
"emprize, or in this mead-hall to meet my death-day."
To the lady the words were well-liking, the vaunt-speech 640
of the Goth; she walked gold-arrayed, high-born queen
of the nation, to sit by her lord.

Then was again as erst within the hall the lofty
word outspoken, the company was happy, the sound
was that of a mighty people; until that sudden the
son of Healfdene was minded to retire to his nightly
rest; he knew that against the high Hall war was
determined by the monster, from the time when they
could [not] see the sun's light or shrouding night came
over all, and the creatures of darkness came stalking 650
abroad; he warred in obscurity. All the company arose.
Then did man greet man, Hrothgar greeted Beowulf,
bespake him luck, mastery in the house of hospitality;
and delivered this speech: " Never before, since I could
" heave hand and shield, did I confide the guard-house

"of the Danes to any man, but only to thee now on this
"occasion. Have now and hold the best of houses;
660 "resolve on success: show valour amain; be vigilant
"against the foe! Thou shalt not have any desire
"unfulfilled, if thou that mighty work with life achievest."

X.

**Beowulf doffs his armour, and watches unarmed. A
point of honour. His companions sleep.**

So Hrothgar, chief of Scyldings, took his departure
with retinue of men, out of hall; he was minded to join
Wealhtheow his queen and consort. The Glory of
kings had—so men told one another—set up a hall-
warden against Grendel; he had undertaken the single
service about the patriarch of the Danes, offered watch
against the monster;—assuredly the Gothic Leed with
670 joyous mien trusted in valorous might and the smile of
Providence.

Then put he off from him his iron byrnie, helmet
from head; delivered to his esquire the richly-
dight sword, choicest steel; and charged him with the
care of his war-harness. Then did the valiant man
Beowulf the Goth utter some vaunting words ere he
mounted on bed: "I reckon myself to be in the fury
"of battle, in warlike feats, no wise below the preten-
"sions of Grendel; for that reason I will not with
680 "sword give him his quietus, deprive him of life,
"although I very well may. Nought knoweth he of
"those gentle practices, to give and take sword-cuts, to
"hew the shield; dread though he be in feats of horror:
"—but we twain shall in the night-time supersede

"the blade, if he dare to court war without weapon;
"and thereafter may the Allwise God, the holy Lord,
"adjudge success on which side soever may to him
"appear meet!"

Then the daring warrior laid him down; the pillow
received the countenance of the eorl; and round about
him many a smart sea-warrior couched to his hall- 690
rest. Not one of them thought that from that
place he should ever again visit his own estate, his
folk and castle, where he was brought up; but they
had been informed that before now a bloody death
had all too much reduced them, the Danish people, in
that festive hall. But to them, the Leeds of Wedermark, did the Lord grant webs of war-speed, strength
and support, that they by the force of one, by his single
prowess, should all be victorious over their foe. For a 700
truth it is shewn, that the mighty God has governed
mankind in every age!

He came in dim night, marching along, ranger of the
dark. The defenders slept, they whose duty it was to
guard that gabled mansion—all slept but one!

It was very well known to all men, that the ruthless
destroyer might not against the will of God whirl them
under darkness; but (all the same) he, vigilant in
defiance of the foe, awaited in full-fraught mood the
arbitrament of battle.

XI.

Grendel's last meal. The battle begins.

710 Then came Grendel marching from the moor under
the misty brows ; he bore the wrath of God.   The
assassin meant to catch some one of human-kind in that
lofty hall ; he tore along under heaven in the direction
where he knew the hospitable building, the gold-hall of
men, metal-spangled, ever ready for his entertainment ;
—that was not the first time he had visited Hrothgar's
homestead.   Never had he in his life-days, earlier or
later, met so tough a warrior, such hall-guards !
720 Came then journeying to the hall the felon mirth-
bereft ; suddenly the door, fastened with bars of wrought
iron, sprang open as soon as he touched it with his
hands ; thus bale-minded and big with rage he wrecked
the vestibule of the hall.   Quickly after that the fiend
was treading on the paven floor ; he went raven-
ing ; out of his eyes there stood likest to flame an
eerie light.   He perceived in the hall many warriors, a
730 troop of kinsmen, grouped together, a band of cousins,
asleep.   Then was his mood exalted to laughter ; he
counted, the fell ruffian, that he should sever, ere day
came, the life of each one of them from his body, seeing
that luck had favoured him to gratify his slaughterous
appetite.   That was not however so destined, that he
should be permitted to eat any more of mankind after
that night.

Mighty rage the kinsman of Hygelac curbed, considering how the assassin meant to proceed in the
course of his ravenings.   Nor was the marauder

minded to delay it; but he seized promptly at 740
his first move a sleeping warrior, tore him in a
moment, crunched the bony frame, drank blood of
veins, swallowed huge morsels; in a trice he had
devoured the lifeless body, feet, hands, and all. He
stepped up nearer forward; he was then taking with
his hand the great-hearted warrior on his bed. The
fiend reached towards him with his fang;—he
promptly seized with shrewd design and grappled
his arm. Quickly did the boss of horrors discover 750
that, that never in all the world, all the quarters of
the earth, had he met man more strange with bigger
hand-grip; he in mood became alarmed in spirit; but
never the quicker could he get away. His mind was to
be going; he wanted to flee into darkness; rejoin the
devils' pack; his entertainment there was not such
as he before had met with in bygone days. Then did
the brave kinsman of Hygelac remember his discourse
of the evening; up he stood full length, and grappled 760
with him amain; his fingers cracked as they would
burst. The monster was making off, the eorl followed
him up. The oaf was minded, if so be he might, to
fling himself loose, and away therefrom to flee into fen-
hollows; he knew that the control of his fingers was
in the grip of a terrible foe; that was a rash expedition which the devastator had made to Heorot!

The Guard-hall roared;—upon all the Danes, upon
the inhabiters of the castle, upon every brave man,
upon the eorlas, came mortal panic. Furious were both 770
the maddened champions, the building resounded; it
was a great wonder that the genial saloon endured the
combatants, that it did not fall to ground, that fair

E

ornament of the country; only that it was inwardly and outwardly so firmly besmithied with iron staunchions of masterly skill! There, from the sill started—as my story tells—many a mead-bench adorned with gold, where the terrible ones contended. Thereanent had the Scylding senators weened at the first, that never would any man by mortal force be able to wreck it, 780 the beautiful and ivoried house, or by craft to disjoint it;—leastwise fire's embrace should swallow it up in vapoury reek.

The noise rose high, with renewed violence; the north-Danes were stricken with eldritch horror every one, whosoever heard even out on the wall the doleful cry, the adversary of God yelling a dismal lay, a song unvictorious: -the thral of hell howling for his wound. 790 He held him too fast, he who was in main the strongest of men in the day of this life.

XII.

Grendel's flight. His arm remains with Beowulf, and is set up as a trophy. Heorot is purged.

The shelter of eorlas was not by any means minded to let the murderous visitant escape alive; he did not reckon his life-days useful to any one of the Leeds. There did many an eorl of Beowulf's unsheath his old heirloom;—would rescue the life of their master, their great captain; if so be they might. They knew it not, —when they plunged into the fight, the stouthearted 800 companions, and thought to hack him on every side, reach his life,—that no choicest blade upon earth, no war-bill would touch that destroyer, but he had by enchantment secured himself against victorious weapons, edges of all kinds. His life-parting [in the day of this life] was destined to be woeful, and the outcast spirit must travel far off into the realm of fiends. Then discovered he that, he who erst in wanton mood had wrought huge atrocity upon mankind 810 —he was out of God's peace—that his body was not at his command, but the valiant kinsman of Hygelac had got hold of him by the hand ; to either was the other's life loathsome. A deadly wound the foul warlock got ; on his shoulder the fatal crack appeared ; the sinews sprang wide, the bone-coverings burst. To Beowulf was victory given ; Grendel must flee life-sick there- 820 from to the coverts of the fen, must make for a cheerless habitation ;—full well he knew that the end of his life was reached, the number of his days. All the Danes had in the issue of that dire struggle the fulfilment of their desire.

He had then purged, he who but now came from far, sagacious and resolute, Hrothgar's hall ; he had rescued it from danger ; had succeeded in his night-task with brilliant achievement. The Leed of the Gothic com- panions had made good his vaunt to the east-Danes ; likewise he had entirely remedied the horror, the 830 harrowing sorrow, which they were enduring before, and of dire necessity were forced to suffer ;—huge indignity. That was a token conspicuous, when the hero of battle had affixed the hand, arm, and shoulder —that was the whole affair of Grendel's fang—under the gabled roof.

XIII.

Horsemen upon Grendel's track.   Riding, racing, and
tale-telling. Beowulf's adventure a minstrel's theme ;—
his fame coupled with Sigemund's, contrasted with
Heremod's.

Then was in the morning—so goes my story—about
the gift-hall many a warrior ; the chiefs of the folk came
840 from far and near, through divers ways, to survey the
prodigy, the traces of the loathed one.   His life-ending
was no grief whatever to any of those who surveyed
the track of the vanquished, how he in doleful mood
away from that place, in buffets worsted, had, death-
doomed and fugitive, fled in mortal terror to the Nicers'
mere.   There was the face of the lake surging with
blood, the gruesome plash of waves all turbid with
850 reeking gore, with sword-spilth ;— the death-doomed
(Grendel) had discoloured it ;—presently he, void of joyance, in fenny covert yielded up his life, his heathen
soul ; there did Hela receive him.

Thence back home went the old Companions along
with many a bachelor from the pleasure-trip ; from
the Mere in high spirits riding on horses, barons on
jennets. There was Beowulf's achievement rehears-
ed ; many a one often said that south nor north between
the seas all the wide world over, other none of shield-
860 bearing warriors under the compass of the firmament
preferable were or worthier of sovereignty.   They did
not however at all disparage their natural lord, gracious
Hrothgar ; but he was a good King !
Now and then the gallant warriors loosened their

russet nags for a gallop, to run a match, where the turfways looked fair, or were favourably known. Otherwhiles a thane of the king's, bombastic groom, his mind full of ballads, the man who remembered good store of old-world tales—word followed 870 word by the bond of truth—began anon to rehearse, cunningly to compose, the adventure of Beowulf, and fluently to pursue the story in its order, with interlacing words. At large he detailed, what he had heard say of Sigemund's exploits, much that was strange, the battle-toil of the Wælsing, distant expeditions, things the sons of men quite knew not of, feud and atrocity ; —none but Fitela by his side, when he would say aught 880 of such matter, uncle to nephew, as they had ever stood by one another in every struggle : they had with swords laid low many of the monster brood. To Sigemund there sprang up after his death-day no little fame ; forasmuch as he, hardy in fight, had quelled the Dragon, the keeper of treasure ; he, the son of a prince, in under the hoary rock, single-handed enterprized the perilous deed ;—Fitela was not with him. Nathless he 890 succeeded so well that the sword sped through the stupendous worm, till it stuck in the bank, noble iron ! the dragon died the death. The champion had by valour attained that he might enjoy the jewel-hoard at his own discretion ; he laded the sea-boat, the son of Wæls bore to the bosom of the ship the bright ornaments ; the Worm dissolved with heat. He was by daring exploits the most famous of adventurers far and 900 wide over the world, shelter of warriors ; such eminence he won.

When Heremod's warfare had slackened, his puis-

sance and emprize, he among the Eotens was de-
coyed forth into the power of enemies, promptly sent
out of the way. Him did billows of sorrow disable too
long; he to his Leeds, to all his princes, became a loyal
anxiety. Moreover, in his earlier times, many a wise
countryman had often deplored the adventurous life of
the ardent soul, such a one as had trusted to him for
910 remedy of grievances, that the royal child might grow
powerful, succeed to the state of his fathers, protect the
people, the treasure and the castle, realm of heroes,
patrimony of the Scyldings. There was he, Hygelac's
kinsman, to all mankind, and to his friends, more
acceptable; the other was seized with fury.

At intervals racing they with their horses measured
the fallow streets. Then was the light of morning
launched and advanced; there was many a varlet
920 going eager-minded to the lofty Hall to see the strange
prodigy;—likewise the king himself from his domestic
lodge, keeper of jewelled hoards, trod with glorious
mien, gorgeously distinguished in the midst of a great
retinue;—and his queen with him, measured the path to
the mead-hall with a bevy of ladies.

XIV.

A patriarchal thanksgiving. Beowulf's account of the fray. Effect upon Unferth.

Hrothgar uttered speech he was going to Hall;
he stood on the Staple; he beheld the steep roof gold-
glittering, and the hand of Grendel.

"For this spectacle a thanksgiving to the Almighty
"be done without delay! Much despite I endured,

"capturings by Grendel; always can God work won- 930
" der after wonder, the Lord of Glory! It was but
"now that I thought I should never see a remedy
"for any of my woes, while the best of houses stood
"blood-stained, soaked in slaughter; the woe had
"scattered all my senators, as men who weened not
"that they ever should rescue the national edifice of
"my Leeds from the hateful ones, the demons and
"bogles.

" Now hath a lad, through might of God, achieved 940
"the deed which we all erewhile were unable with our
"wisdom to compass. Lo! that may she say, what
"lady soever mothered that child by human genera-
"tion, if yet she liveth, that to her was the Ancient
"Master favourable in her child-bearing!

" Now I will heartily love thee, Beowulf, youth most
"excellent, as if thou wert my son; from this time
"forth keep thou up the new relation. There shall be
"no lack to thee of any desires in the world, so far as I 950
"have power. Full oft have I for less service decreed
"recompense, honour from the treasury, to a less dis-
"tinguished hero, less prompt to fight.

" Thou thyself hast by deeds achieved, that thy fame
"will live ever and always. May the Almighty reward
"thee with good, as he hath just now done!"

Beowulf uttered speech, Ecgtheow's son: "We
"discharged that high task, fighting with right good
"heart; shrewdly we enterprized the terror of the 960
"unknown. I'd a liked it vastly better, that thou'dst
"a seen his very self, the fiend in full gear, ready to
"drop. I thought quickly to fix him on a bloody bed
"with hard grapplings, that he for my hand-grip should

"lie death-struggling, unless his body vanished ; I could
"not, as the Ancient would not, baulk his passage ; I
"did not stick close enough to him, the man-queller ;
970 "the fiend was too over-mighty in his making off.
"However he left his fist—to save his life and mark
"his track—his arm and shoulder : not thereby how-
"ever has the wretched being bought reprieve ; none
"the longer will he live, the loathsome pest burthened
"with crimes ; but the wound hath him, in deadly grip
"close pinioned, in baleful bands ; in that condition
"must he, crime-stained wretch, abide the great doom,
"according as the Ancient One may will to assign his
"portion."

980   A silenter man was then the son of Ecglaf in the brag
of martial exploits ; since it was by the hero's valour the
ethelings beheld the hand, the fiendish fingers, over the
high roof, every one straight before him.   Each one of
the nail-places was likest to steel, hand-spur of the
heathenish marauder, horrible spikes ; every one declared there was nothing so hard would graze them, no
sword of old celebrity that would take off the monster's
990 bloody war-fist.

XV.

Heorot restored.   Rejoicings and giving of gifts.

Then was order promptly given that the interior of
Heorot should be decorated ; many they were, of men
and of women, who garnished that genial palace, hospitable hall.   Gold-glistering shone the brocaded tapes-
tries along the walls, pictures many for the wonder of
all people who have an eye for such.   That bright

building was terribly wrecked in its whole interior,
though it had been strengthened with iron fastenings;
the hinges were wrenched away; the roof alone had
escaped altogether unhurt, when the destroyer, stained 1000
with atrocities, took to flight in desperation of life.

It is not easy to elude [death], try it who will; but
every living soul of the sons of men, of dwellers upon
ground, must of necessity approach the destined spot,
where his body, bedded in fast repose, shall sleep after
supper.

Then was the time and the moment, that Healfdene's
son should go to Hall; the king was minded himself to 1010
share the feast. Never that I heard of did that nation
in stronger force about their bounty-giver more bravely
muster. They went to bench in merry guise—while
their kinsmen enjoyed the copious feast, and with fair
courtesy quaffed many a mead-bowl—mighty men in
the lofty hall, Hrothgar and Hrothulf. The interior of
Heorot was wholly filled with friends; no treachery
had imperial Scyldings at that early date attempted.

Then did the son of Healfdene present to Beowulf a
golden ensign in reward of victory, decorated staff- 1020
banner, helmet and mail-coat; many beheld when they
brought the grand treasure-sword before the hero.
Beowulf tasted the beaker on the hall-floor; no need
had he to be ashamed of that bounty-giving before the
archers. I heard not many instances of men giving to
other at ale-bench four treasures gold-bedight in
friendlier wise. About the helmet's roof the crest was 1030
fastened with wire-bound fencing for the head, in order
that file-wrought war-scoured blades might not cruelly

scathe it, when the shielded fighter had to go against angry foes.

Then did the Shelter of eorlas command to bring eight horses gold-cheeked into the court within the palings; on one of them stood the saddle gaily caparisoned and decorated with silver, which was the war-seat of the high king, when the son of Healfdene
1040 was minded to exercise the play of swords;—never failed in the front the charger of the famous (king) when the slain were falling. And then did the chief of the Ingwines deliver unto Beowulf possession of both at once, both horses and arms;—bade him enjoy them well. So manfully did the illustrious chieftain, the hoard-warden of heroes, reward battle-risks with horses and treasures, so as never will any mispraise them who is minded to speak sooth according to right.

XVI.

Gifts to Beowulf's comrades. Music and Song. The Lay of Hnæf, relating the consequences of Finn's treachery.

Moreover, to each one of those who had made the
1050 voyage with Beowulf, did the Captain of warriors give a precious gift at the mead-bench, an old heir-loom; and gave orders to compensate with gold for that (missing) one, that one whom Grendel had atrociously killed, as he would have killed more of them, had not the providence of God, had not Wyrd, stood in his way;—and, the courage of that man. The Ancient One ruled then, as he now and alway doth, over all persons of human race; therefore is prudence each-
1060 where best, fore-cast of soul. Much experience of

pleasant and of painful must he make, who long here
in these struggling days brooks the world.

Then was song and instrumental music together
blended, concerning Healfdene's war-chief,—the harp
was struck, a ballad often recited, what time the hall-
joy along the mead-bench was invoked by Hrothgar's
minstrel—concerning the sons of Finn, when the
alarm overtook them: "A mighty man of the half-
"Danes, Hnæf the Scylding,.................
"was doomed to fall in the Frisian conflict.   1070

"Hildeburh however had no cause to extol the fide-
"lity of the Eotens; without her fault she was in the
"clash of shields bereft of those dear to her, sons and
"brother; they fell one after another wounded with
"the spear;—that was a doleful princess. Not without
"cause did the daughter of Hôc bewail the sad event
"when morning came, and she in full daylight could
"see the carnage of her kin, where she had till now
"enjoyed the world's best happiness.   1080

"Battle had destroyed all Finn's thanes, save a few
"only,.so that he could not, on the place of debate,
"against Hengest at all contend, nor rescue the sad
"remnant of his men from the hostility of the king's
"thane; but they (the Frisians) proffered him (Hengest)
"conditions of peace, that they would wholly yield to
"him the possession of another mansion, hall, and high
"seat, so that they (the Danes) might share equal posses-
"sion of it with the sons of the Eotens, and at money-
"givings the son of Folcwalda (i. e. Finn) should day 1090
"by day honour the Danes, should gratify with rings
"the troop of Hengest, with metallic wealth of beaten
"gold, in exactly the same measure as he purposed in

"the festive hall to encourage the Frisians born.
"Thereupon they ratified on the two sides a fast
"treaty of peace; Finn engaged, loyally and un-
"reservedly, with oaths to Hengest, that he would
"govern that sad remnant by constituted law in all
1100 "honour; so that not any man of them, by word or
"work, should break the treaty; nor with guileful
"intent ever mention make, though they (the Danes)
"had followed their patron's banesman, when bereaved
"of a lord, seeing that they were by necessity driven to
"it. If on the other hand any of the Frisians with
"aggressive speech were recalling the blood-feud, it
"should be atoned by the edge of the sword. The
"oath it was sworn, and massive gold was hoisted out
"of the treasury.

"Of the warlike Scyldings the best campaigner was
1110 "on the fire-heap ready; at the pyre was conspicuous
"the blood-stained sark, the swine all gilded, the boar
"of hard iron, many a noble wounded to death; --
"several had fallen in the struggle. Orders were given
"by Hildeburh, that at Hnæf's pyre her own son
"should be committed to flame, that the body should be
"burnt and placed on the bale-fire. The poor lady
"wailed on his shoulder, she uttered her grief in
"lamentations; the war-hero passed up in flame, soared
1120 "to the clouds. Hugest of corpse-fires, it roared on its
"eminence; heads wasted away, wound-gates did burst;
"then sprang blood from the place where the body had
"been cruelly assaulted. The fire devoured them all—
"greediest of demons—all of those whom war had there
"destroyed, of both peoples; their bloom was departed.

XVII.

The remainder of the Lay of Hnæf. A picture of social pleasure. Speech of the queen to the king.

"The warriors departed to visit their dwellings, bereft
"of friends to re-visit Friesland, their homesteads and
"head-borough. Hengist however during that blood-
"stained winter tarried with Finn, loyally and without
"cavil; his home he thought of, though he was not able 1130
"to drive over the sea his ring-prowed ship; the holm
"surged with storm, battled with wind; winter locked
"the wave with icy barrier; until that the next year
"came to town, as even now it continues to do; and
"those punctual time-keepers, the days of glorious
"weather. Then was winter gone, the bosom of the
"earth was fair; the adventurer was astir, the guest
"forward to quit hospitable courts.

"He however (Hengest) thought more on revenge
"than on sea-voyaging, if he could bring about a 1140
"collision, that he might therein remember the sons
"of the Eotens. So (the better to hide his thought) he
"did not decline military brotherhood, when Hun laid
"upon his breast (the sword) Lafing, luminary of battle,
"best of blades; the edges of that sword were famous
"among the Eotens. Consequently the savage-minded
"Finn was by and bye overtaken by glib sword-bale at
"his own manor; when once Guthlaf and Oslaf, off their
"sea-voyage, made sore mention of the grim assault,
"brought up a deal of wrongs; he could not refrain 1150
"his wild rage in his breast. Then was the hall be-
"dight with embattled corpses;—likewise Finn was

"slain, the king in the midst of his guard, and the
"queen taken. The archers of the Scyldings con-
"veyed to their ships the whole establishment of the
"king of the country, whatsoever they at Finn's Hám
"could find of jewels and curious gems. On the sea-path
"they conveyed the courtly ladies to the Danes, brought
"them to their Leeds." The Lay was sung to its end,
1160 the minstrel's descant.

Enjoyment rose high as before, bright was the sound
of revelry, the drawers served wine out of curious
flagons. Then came Wealhtheow forward, moving under
her golden diadem, to where the two brave men sate,
uncle and nephew; up to that time was their natural
affection undisturbed, either to other true. Likewise
there Unferth the speaker sate at the feet of the
Scyldings' lord; every man of them trusted his spirit
that he had great courage, though he had not been loyal
to his kindred at sword-play.

Spake then the lady of the Scyldings:—"Receive
1170 "this beaker, sovereign mine, wealth-dispenser! be thou
"merry, a munificent friend of men, and speak to the
"Goths with comfortable words. So it behoves one to
"do! Near and far, thou now hast peace! To me it
"hath been said, that thou wouldest have the hero for
"thy son. Heorot is purged, the bright ring-hall;
"dispense whilst thou mayest many bounties;—and to
"thy children leave folk and realm, when thou must
1180 "away to see Eternity. I know my gracious Hrothulf
"that he will honourably govern the younger ones, if
"thou earlier than he, O friend of the Scyldings,
"quittest the world. I think that he will repay our
"children with good, if he that fully remembers,

"what gracious attentions thou and I bestowed for
"his comfort and advantage in the time past when
"he was an infant." She turned then towards the bench
where her boys were, Hréthric and Hróthmund, and
the sons of mighty men, the youth all together; there 1190
the brave man sate, Beowulf of the Goths, by the
two brothers.

XVIII.

Gifts of the queen to the hero, and her speech to him. The hall is arranged as a dormitory.

To him the cup was borne; and friendly invitation
(to drink) was offered with words; and twisted gold
was graciously presented, armlets two, a mantle and
rings; the grandest of carcanets that I have heard of
on earth. None superior among the treasures of men
heard I ever of under heaven, since Hama bore away
to the bright fortress the necklace of the Brisings— 1200
jewel and casket; he fled the toils of Eormanric;
chose eternal counsel.

That collar had Hygelac of the Goths, grandson (or
nephew) of Swerting, on his latest expedition, when
under his flag he defended his prize, guarded the spoil;
him Fate took off, when he for wantonness challenged
woe, feud with the Frisians; he carried that decoration,
the costly stones over the wave-bowl, the mighty chieftain; he fell shield in hand; so then came into the power 1210
of the Franks the corpse of the king, the breast apparel,
and the collar along with the res. : inferior combatants
stripped the slain by the fortune of war; the people
of the Goths tenanted the bed of death.—The Hall
echoed with sound (of Music).

Wealhtheo uttered speech; she spake before that company: "Brook this collar, Beowulf, beloved youth, "with luck, and make use of this mantle; stately pos- "sessions; and prosper well; make thyself famous by 1220 "valour, and to these boys be thou a kind adviser! " I will reward thee for it. Thou hast attained, that far "and near, for all future time, men will celebrate thee, "even as widely as the sea encircleth windy walls. Be "thou, whilst thou live, a happy prince! With good will " I accord thee precious possessions. Be thou to my son "loyal with deeds, sustaining joyance. Here is each "warrior to other true, kindly disposed, loyal to their 1230 "chief; the thanes are obedient, the people all ready! " Retainers be merry, do as I bid you."

She went then to her chair. There was high festivity; men drank wine, Wyrd they knew not, the cruel destiny, as it had gone forth, for many a noble. By and bye the evening came, and Hrothgar betook him to his lodge, the prince to his repose.

Countless nobles guarded the Hall, as they had often done in earlier time: they cleared away the bench- 1240 boards; it was strewn throughout with beds and bolsters. One of the revellers, whose end was near, lay down to rest in hall a doomed man. At their heads they set the shields, the bright bucklers; there on the bench was over each etheling, plain to be seen, the towering war-helmet, the ringéd mail-coat, the shaft of awful power. Their custom was that they were constantly ready for war, whether at home or in the field, in both cases alike, whatever the occasion on which their liege lord had need of their services;— 1250 it was a good people.

THE SECOND PART.

XIX.

In the night the old water-hag comes, seizes one of the
sleepers, and fetches away Grendel's arm.   Beowulf is
hastily summoned to the king at early dawn.

So they sank down to sleep.   One there was who
sorely paid for that night's rest, in the manner that had
very often happened to them, since Grendel had occupied the gold-hall, had perpetrated violence, until his
end arrived, death after crimes.   That became manifest, widely known to men, that an avenger still lived
after the (slain) foe ; long to remember the disaster ;
Grendel's mother, beldam troll-wife, thought of her
desolation, creature that had to dwell in the dreari- 1260
ness of water, cold streams, ever since Cain was the
knife-bane of his only brother, his father's son ; he then
went forth an outlaw, marked with murder, shunning
human society; he kept the wilderness.   Thence grew a
number of branded creatures ;—one of those was Grendel, horrible ban-wolf; he at Heorot found a vigilant
man waiting for battle.   There did the monster grapple
with him ; he however remembered the strength of his 1270
might, the marvellous gift which God had given to him,
and he trusted to the Supreme for grace, courage, and
support ; therefore he overcame the fiend, subdued the
hellish demon ; so he departed crest-fallen, void of
joyance, to see his death-place, foe of man.   And yet his

G

mother, nevertheless, bloodthirsty and gallows-minded, was going to enter upon a sorrow-fraught way to wreak the death of her son.

So the hag came to Heorot, where the jewelled Danes 1280 slept throughout the Hall. Then was it for the eorlas a sudden upset, when Grendel's mother burst into their midst. The terror was less (i. e. than the terror of Grendel) just in the same proportion as female strength, woman's war-terror, is (of less account) with an armed man; when the well-hafted steel, hammer-toughened, the bloodstained sword, with edge effective, sheareth resisting boar on helmet. Then was the hard-edged sword drawn throughout the benches, many a wide buckler raised firm in hand; many one thought 1290 not of helmet, nor of spacious byrnie, when the alarm surprized him.

The hag was in a hurry; it wanted to get out from there with life, because it was discovered; promptly it had seized one of the ethelings tight, and then it went to fen. That man was to Hrothgar, in quality of comrade, dearest of warriors between the seas, mighty shield-combatant;—him the hag crushed in his sleep, illustrious baron. Beowulf was not there; 1300 but another lodging had been assigned, after the gift-giving, to the distinguished Goth. A cry was heard in Heorot; the blood-sprent hag took away the well-known hand; anxiety was renewed, was set up in the castle. That barter was not good, which they on both sides were compelled to pay for with lives of friends.

Then was the venerable king, the hoary man of war, in embittered mood, when he knew that his chiefest

thane no longer lived, that the man most dear to him
was dead.   Hastily to (the king's) bower was Beowulf 1310
fetched, the victorious stripling.   At early dawn, he
went with his warriors, the noble champion, he and his
comrades, where the sapient king was waiting to be
resolved, whether the Almighty will ever, after the spell
of woe, bring about a change.   He then marched along
the flooring, the expedite man, with his little band,—
hall-timbers echoed—until he accosted with words the
wise lord of the Ingwines, and enquired if, according to
his sincere wish, he had had a restful night.   1320

XX.

Hrothgar's answer to Beowulf's morning salutation; he
    deplores the fate of Æschere; and describes the haunt
    of the water-demons.

Hrothgar, crown of Scyldings, uttered speech : "Ask
"not thou after welfare ! Grief is renewed for the
"Danish Leeds. Æschere is dead, Yrmenlaf's elder
"brother, my secretary and my counsellor; my body-
"squire, when we in battle defended our heads, what
"time foot-fighters closed, boar-crests clashed ;—such
"should a warrior be, a long-tried etheling, such as
"Æschere was.   In Heorot hath he met his death at 1330
"the hands of the raging destroyer; I know not in
"what direction the gruesome corpse-exulting thing
"took its return-way leaving tracks of its forage.   She
"hath wreaked the feud, for that thou yesternight didst
"quell Grendel in masterful wise with stern grapplings ;
"for that he too long had wasted and destroyed my
"people.   He in fight succumbed with forfeiture of life ;

"and now hath come the other, a mighty ravager,
1340 "would avenge her kin;—yea hath further aggravated
"the feud, as may well appear to many a thane, who
"along with his sovereign groans in spirit, in cruel
"heart-grief; now the hand of him who was the pro-
"moter of all your desires lies still in death.

　"That I did hear say by land-owners, Leeds of mine,
"heads of Halls, that they saw a pair of such, huge
"mark-stalkers, keeping the moors, creatures of strange
1350 "fashion; one of them was, according to the clearest
"they could make out, a beldam's likeness, the other
"miscreated thing trod lonely tracks in man's figure;
"only he was huger than any other man; him in old
"times the country folk used to call Grendel: they know
"not about any father, whether they had any in pedigree
"before them of mysterious goblins.　They inhabit
"unvisited land, wolf-crags, windy bluffs, the dread fen-
1360 "track, where the mountain waterfall amid precipitous
"gloom vanisheth beneath, flood under earth; not far
"hence it is, reckoning by miles, that the Mere standeth,
"and over it hang rimy groves; a wood with clenchèd
"roots overshrouds the water.　There may every night
"a fearful portent be seen, fire on the flood; none so
"wise liveth of the children of men as to know the
"depth.　Though the heath-roamer, when exhausted by
"hounds, the hart strong in his horns, make for the
1370 "wood-coverts, driven from afar; sooner will he resign
"his breath, his life on the bank, sooner than he will
"there in plunge his head.　That is no comfort-
"able place; therefrom mount up the raging waves,
"murky to the clouds, when wind stirreth foul weather,
"till the air thickens, the skies crack.　Now is it

"again to thee alone that we look for counsel! The
"haunt as yet thou knowest not, the dreadful place,
"where thou mayest find the guilty felon; go for it
"if thou dare! I will recompense thee for that warfare 1380
"with treasure, with old stored wealth, as I did before,
"with coilèd gold, if thou comest away."

XXI.

Beowulf soothes the king, and gaily undertakes the new
adventure. The cavalcade to the Mere. The look of
it. Beowulf arms ; his sword is described.

Beowulf son of Ecgtheow uttered speech : "Sorrow
"not experienced Sire! better is it for every man that
"he should avenge his friend, than that he should
"greatly mourn. Every one of us must look for
"the end of worldly life; he who has the chance
"should achieve renown before death; that is for a
"mighty man, when life is past, the best memorial.
"Rouse thee, guardian of the kingdom! let us promptly 1390
"set forth to explore the route of Grendel's kin. I
"vow it to thee; he shall by no means escape to
"covert; neither in the bowels of the earth, nor in
"the haunted wood, nor in ocean's depth—go where
"he will! This day have thou patience of all thy
"woes, as I have high confidence in thy behalf."
Up sprang then the aged (king); he thanked God,
the mighty Lord, for what that man had spoken.
Then Hrothgar's horse was bridled, the crull-maned 1400
charger. The wise monarch rode forth stately; the
foot-force marched, of shield-bearing men. Traces

there were broadly visible along the slopes of the
weald, the track (of the foe) over the grounds; right
forward (the warlock) had gone, over the murky moor,
it had carried off, lifeless, the most beloved of kindred
thanes, of those who kept home with Hrothgar.

Then did the Scion of ethelings pass lightly over steep
1410 stone-banks, narrow gullies, strait lonesome paths, an
untravelled route, sheer bluffs, many habitations of
nicors. He with few companions, practised men, went
forward to explore the ground, until that he of a sudden
perceived the gloomy trees overhanging the grisly rock,
a joyless wood; beneath it was a standing water, dreary
and troubled. All the Danes, all the friends of the
Scyldings, had a shock of feeling, many a thane had to
1420 suffer; horror seized each warrior, when on that lake-
cliff they came across the head of Æschere. The pool
seethed with blood—the folk beheld it—with hot gore.

The horn sounded from time to time a spirited bugle-
blast. The troop all sate them down; there saw they
along the water many things of serpent kind, monstrous
sea-snakes at their swimming gambols; and likewise on
the jutting slopes nicors lying, those that in the early
hours of the morning often procure disastrous going
1430 on the sailroad; dragons and strange beasts:—they
tumbled away, spitish and rage-blown; they had caught
sound of the racket, the clarion's clang. The Leed of
the Goths with an arrow out of his bow detached one
of them from life, and from all future swimming
matches; insomuch that in his vitals stood fixed the
inexorable war-shaft; he in the element was the slacker
at swimming, from the circumstance that death had
caught him. Promptly was he on the waves with

boar-poles harpoon-armed, tightly nipped—barred of his tricks—and landed on the point, the prodigious 1440 wave-tosser ;—the men beheld the grisly goblin.

Beowulf geared himself in knightly armour ; in no wise was he anxious for his life ; now must the war-byrnie, hand-woven, spacious and decorated, make trial of swimming ; the byrnie which knew to protect the body, that his breast, his life, might not be scathed by the grip of battle, the spiteful clutch of the furious one. Moreover the white helmet guarded his head, the helmet that was to plunge into the depths of the pool, to face buffeting waters, with all its decoration of 1450 silver, encircled with princely wreathings, as a weapon-smith in ancient days wrought it, wonderfully executed it, set it round with boar figures, so that never might brand nor war-blades make any impression upon it.

That moreover was not the least important of helps to his valour, which Hrothgar's orator lent to him at his need ;—the name of that hafted blade was Hrunting, it was preeminently one of old heirlooms ;— the edge was iron, mottled with poison-twigs, hardened 1460 with battle-gore ; never had it in conflict proved false to any man who brandished it with hands, such man as durst adventure on paths of terror, where nations meet as foes ; that was not the first occasion that it had been required to discharge heroic work. Manifestly Ecglaf's son, of doughty puissance, remembered not what he had recently uttered when flushed with wine, seeing now he made loan of that weapon to a rarer sword-gallant ;—for himself he durst not adventure his life among the turmoil of waves, to fulfil mastery ;— 1470 there he fell short of glory, of high achievement.   It was not so with the other, when he had harnessed him for combat.

XXII.

Beowulf's nuncupatory will.   He plunges into the abyss, and meets the troll-wife.   The battle begins.

Beowulf son of Ecgtheow uttered speech: " Bethink "thee now, great son of Healfdene, sapient monarch, "now I am ready to start, oh thou gold-friend of men, "what we two lately talked of;—If I in thy service "had to quit life, that thou to me wouldest ever be, 1480 "after my departure, in the place of a father;—be thou "protector to my kindred thanes, my familiar comrades, "if Hild should take me; in such a case do thou, "beloved Hrothgar, forward the presents which thou "hast given me, to Hygelac. So will the Master of "the Goths be able to understand by that gold, "Hrethel's son will be able to see for himself when he "gazeth upon that treasure, that I had found a boun- "tifully good distributor of jewels, and was in luck "while my fortune lasted. And do thou let Unferth "have the ancient heir-loom, the curious damasked 1490 "sword; let the far-famed man have Hardedge; I will "with Hrunting achieve for myself renown, or death "shall take me."

After these words the leed of the Weder-Goths dashed bravely off, would await no answer;—the eddying flood engulphed the warrior. It was then a main while of the day ere he could reach the country at the bottom.

Soon was that perceived by the blood-thirsty crea- ture, grim and greedy, which for a hundred seasons

had kept the watery region, that one of the children of
men was exploring from above the habitation of goblins. 1500
It made a grab then towards him ; it caught the brave
man with grisly talons ; nevertheless it pierced not to
wound the wholeness of his body ; ring-mail outside
fenced him about, insomuch that the hag could not get
through that jacket of service, well-knit limb-sark, with
its loathsome fingers. Then did the she-wolf of the
lake, when she came to the bottom, bear the jewelled
prince to her mansion, so that he had no power at all
—courage enough he had—to wield his weapons ; but
so many monsters harassed him in swimming, many 1510
a water-beast with hostile tusks battered his war-sark,
the brigands were in pursuit.

Then did the eorl perceive that he was in some
strange abysmal hall, where no water at all molested
him, nor could the violence of the flood touch him,
being kept off by the roofèd hall ; firelight he saw,
an eerie lustre, shining bright. Then the hero knew
it was the she-wolf of the abyss, the mighty carline of
the Mere ;—onset he delivered with slaughter-bill, his 1520
hand delayed not the stroke, so that about her head the
costly blade resounded a greedy war-song. Then did
the visitor discover that the battle-gleamer would not
bite, not scathe life, but the edge failed the master
at need ; it had in times past supported many encounters, had often cleft helmet, war-harness of the
doomed ;—that was the first time for the honoured
treasure, that its fame broke down. Again he was
for action, in courage never faltering, mindful of ex- 1530
ploits, Hygelac's kinsman. Away did the wrathful
combatant then fling the damascened blade cunningly

bedizened, insomuch that it lay along on the earth, stark and steel-edged ; he trusted to his strength, the hand-grip of his might.

So it behoves a man to act, when he in battle thinks to attain enduring PRAISE ; —he will not be caring about his life.

Then did the Leed of the warlike Goths—nought recked he of deadly peril—seize Grendel's dam by the shoulder ; then did the man valiant in fight, as he was 1540 full of rage, sway his deadly adversary so that she sank on the pavement.   The hag swiftly paid him back reprisal with fell grapplings, and closed in upon him : —then staggered he with spirits exhausted, he the strongest of warriors, the champion-soldier, insomuch that he fell prostrate.   Then did the hag sit upon the visitant of her hall, and drew her knife, broad and brown-edged ; would revenge her bairn, her only off-spring.   About his shoulder lay the breast-net inter-laced ; that fenced his life ; against point and against edge it barred the entrance.

1556   Then had the son of Ecgtheow, the champion of the Goths, miscarried under the vast profound, had not his campaigning byrnie, his hard war-net, afforded help ;—and holy God controlled the victory, the Lord of provi-dence, the heavenly Ruler, he determined it aright, and that with ease ;—presently he again stood erect on his feet.

XXIII.

Beowulf finishes the business. The king's party give
  him up, and go home. Beowulf's comrades remain
  on the cliff. Fidelity rewarded. An after-dinner
  surprize.

Then saw he among the armour a monumental
cutlass, an old cotenish sword, of edge effective, a
trophy of warriors ;—that was the very pride of weapons, only that it was huger than any other man could 1560
bear to the battle-game ; it was good and gallant, hand-
iwork of giants.   Then did he, the champion of the
Scyldings, grasp Fetelhilt ; exasperate and greedy of
fight he drew the jewelled arm ; despairing of his life,
he smote in his fury ; insomuch that the hard steel
caught her by the neck, broke through the bone-rings,
the bill sped all through the doomed flesh-jacket ;--she
dropped on the pavement ; the sword was gory ; the
lad was fain of his work.

The glimmer flashed up, light filled the place, even 1570
as when from heaven serenely shineth the candle of
the firmament.   He scanned the apartment with his eye,
then took his way along by the wall ; stubborn the thane
of Hygelac swung his weapon aloft by the hilt, fierce
and aggressive.   That blade was not flung away by the
hero, but he was forthwith minded to repay Grendel
the many fatal assaults he had wrought on the west-
Danes oftener far than a single once, when he slew 1580
Hrothgar's hearth-comrades in their slumber ; sleeping
men of the Danish folk he devoured fifteen, and an
equal number he conveyed away, hideous spoil.   He
had paid him his recompense for that, the furious

champion had; insomuch that he now beheld him at
rest, weary of war, even Grendel he saw lying, bereft of
life, so deadly for him had erst the conflict at Heorot
been. The carcass gaped wide, when it after death
1590 received the blow, the hard sword-slash; then did
he cut the head from off him.

Forthwith was that perceived by the observant
men who with Hrothgar were watching over the water,
that the wave-plash was all turbid, the surf was
tinged with blood: the men of grizzled locks, the
old men, spake together about the brave man, how that
they expected not the Etheling back again, did not
expect that he would come radiant with victory to seek
the illustrious prince; inasmuch as the more part were
of opinion, that the she-wolf of the mere had torn him in
pieces.

1600 Then came the ninth hour of the day. The impetuous Scyldings quitted the bluff; the gold-friend
of men took his departure homeward thence. The
foreigners sate fast, sick at heart, and upon the pool
they gazed; they wished and did not expect, that they
might ever get sight of their lord and captain in the
body.

Then did that sword begin —under spilth of blood in
fearful clots—the war-bill began to waste away ;—that
was a marvellous thing that it melted all away, likest
to ice when the Father dissolveth the rigour of frost and
1610 unwindeth the ropes of the torrent, he who hath control of times and seasons; that is the true Governor.

The Leed of the Weder-Goths took not of rare
possessions in those halls —though he saw many
there—aught more than the head, and with it the

hilt that was metal-spangled; the sword had already melted away, the decorated weapon had burnt up;—so fiercely hot was that blood, and so venomous the strange goblin which had perished there in that habitation.

Soon was he swimming, he who erst had strugglingly encountered the onset of furious beasts; up through the water he dived; the wave-depths were all purified, 1620 spacious haunts; now that the goblin had quitted life, and this transitory scene.

Then came he to land, the crown of the men from over the sea, bravely swimming;—he exulted in his lake-spoil, in the mighty burthen which he had with him. Then went they to meet him, they thanked God, the valiant band of thanes, they rejoiced over their captain, for that they had been so happy as to get sight of him whole and sound. Then was from the ardent hero his helmet and byrnie promptly slackened :—sullenly the 1630 Mere subsided, water under welkin, dusk with battle-gore.

Forth thence they fared upon the tracks of their (former) march, fain in their souls, they passed over the country, and along the public highways: men of kingly courage bore the head-piece away from the Mere-cliff, toilsomely for every one of them: of the lusty and stalwart fellows four were required to convey with much ado on the gory pole the head of Grendel to the gold-hall; (and so they went) till that unexpectedly to 1640 Hall the brave adventurers arrived, fourteen of Goths marching; their Captain withal, glorious in their midst, trod the grounds of the mead-hall. Then did the Commander of the thanes proceed to enter, deed-keen man, adorned with glory, warlike hero, to accost Hrothgar:

then was Grendel's head borne by the hair into the hall
where men drank ;—startling for the nobles and the
1650 lady withal ; a visage indescribable did men behold.

XXIIII.

**Beowulf reports his experience to Hrothgar, and gives
him the wondrous hilt, which is examined and
described. Hrothgar's paternal discourse.**

Beowulf son of Ecgtheow uttered speech : " Lo and
" behold ! we unto thee, oh son of Healfdene, Leed of
" the Scyldings, have joyfully brought these Mere-spoils
" which thou here lookest on, in token of achievement !
" Not easily did I fight it through with life : in battle
" under water I had hardly faced out the task, well-nigh
" had the struggle failed, only that God shielded me. I
1660 " could not in conflict accomplish aught with Hrunting,
" though that be a good weapon ; but the Ruler of men
" vouchsafed to me that I on the wall saw smilingly
" hanging an old sword of huge size—oftenest hath He
" guided men when they have no other friend—insomuch
" that I grasped at that weapon. Then smote I in
" that campaign—occasion favouring me—the keepers of
" the house. Then did that battle-bill consume away,
" that twisted piece, by reason of that blood which
" gushed forth, hottest of battle-gore ; I brought away
" from the enemy that hilt as a trophy ; I avenged the
1670 " atrocities, the death-agony of Danes, as it was meet.
" Accordingly I promise it to thee that thou in Heorot
" mayest sleep free from care with the regiment of thy
" troopers ; and so may every thane of thy Leeds, of the
" seniority and of the juniority, for that thou needest
" not on their account apprehend danger, O chief of

"Scyldings, in that quarter, life-bale to warriors ; as
"erewhile thou diddest."

Then was the gilded hilt given to the veteran soldier,
the hoary leader in battle, given into his hand, ancient
workmanship of giants ; it passed, after the demons 1680
were quelled, into the possession of the prince of the
Danes, a work of mystic smiths ; and so when the
atrocious creature, God's enemy, murder-criminous, left
this world, and his mother too, it went into the possession of the best of worldly kings between the seas,
of all that ever in Scania distributed wealth.

Hrothgar uttered speech ;—he surveyed the hilt,
the old relic ; upon it was written the origin of the
primæval quarrel, what time the flood, the rushing
ocean, destroyed the giants' brood ; they got for them- 1690
selves a bitter fate ; that was a tribe estranged from the
Eternal Captain, to them did the Ruler assign final
retribution with whelming water. Likewise on the
mounting of sheer gold there was with rune-staves
rightly inscribed, set down, and said, for whom that
sword had erst been wrought, best of steely fabrics,
with wreathen hilt, and dragon ornament.

Then did the wise son of Healfdene utter speech—
all held their peace— : "That, lo ! may a man say, a 1700
"man who promoteth truth and right among folk,—he
"remembereth all long ago, the old housemaster—
"that this eorl was born superior ! The fame is
"spread through distant parts, my friend Beowulf, the
"fame of thee over every nation. Withal thou dost
"carry it modestly, thy prowess with discretion of mind.
"I shall make good to thee my plighted love, according
"as was before said betwixt us two ; thou art destined

"to prove a comfort sure and lasting to thy Leeds, a
"help to mankind.

1710   "Heremod did not prove so to the descendants of
"Ecgwela, to the honourable Scyldings; he waxed
"great not for their pleasure, but for mortal fray and
"for death-blows to the Danish Leeds; he in his un-
"governed mood crushed his boon companions, the
"squires of his body; until that at last he wandered
"forth alone, the illustrious monarch, away from human
"society; notwithstanding that the mighty God had
"with the attractions of strength, with puissance,
"exalted him, promoted him, above all men. Never-
"theless in his soul there grew a blood-thirsty passion;
1720 "—far was he from giving rings to the Danes accord-
"ing to merit; he continued estranged from social joy,
"so that he suffered the penalty of that outrage in the
"settled disaffection of his people.

"Do thou take warning by that; understand the
"ornament of man! It is about thee that I
"being old in years and experience have told
"this tale.

"Wonderful it is to tell, how the mighty God with
"large intelligence dispenses understanding to mankind,
"dispenses position and prowess—he holds the dis-
"position of all things. Sometimes he lets the purpose
"of a man of noble race turn towards possession, he
1730 "giveth to him earthly joy on his estate, to hold the
"citadel of men, he assigns to him regions of the world
"so extensive, a realm so wide, that he in his unwisdom
"is not able to carry his thought to the end of it; he
"dwelleth in prosperity, not anything annoys him, not
"sickness nor age nor carking care darkens his spirits,

"no quarrel on any side, no feud appears; but all the
"world moves to his mind, he knows not reverse.

XXV.

The conclusion of Hrothgar's discourse. More feast-
ing;—and then came bed-time, for which the herò had
huge desire. Beowulf slept till the voice of the bird
proclaimed sunrise. Preparing to return home, he
restores Hrunting to Unferth courteously.

"Until at length within the man himself something 1740
"of arrogancy grows and develops; then sleepeth the
"guardian, the soul's keeper; it is too fast that sleep,
"awfully profound, the assassin is very nigh, he who
"from his arrow-bow malignantly shooteth. Then is
"he, helmeted man, smitten in the breast with a
"bitter shaft: he cannot defend himself from the
"crooked exorbitant counsels of the damnèd sprite; he
"fancies that it is too little, all that he has so long
"enjoyed; he is covetous, and malignant; glorieth
"not in the pomp of bestowing gilded decorations; and 1750
"he forgetteth the ulterior consequences; he too lightly
"considers how that God the Dispenser of glory had
"erewhile given him the post of dignity. Then at the
"end of the chapter it returns to this, that the body
"shrunken falls away, the outgoing life drops;—another
"fills his room, one who ungrudgingly distributes
"treasure, the eorl's old accumulations;—timid pru-
"dence he despises.

"Guard thee against the fatal grudge, beloved
"Beowulf, youth most excellent, and choose for thee
"the better course, enduring counsels! incline not to 1760
I

"arrogancy, thou mighty champion! Now is thy
"strength in full bloom for one while; eftsoons it will
"happen that sickness or sword will bereave thee of
"puissance;--either clutch of fire or whelm of flood,
"either assault of knife or flight of javelin, either
"wretched eld or glance of eyes, will mar and darken
"all ; without more ado it will come to pass that death
"will subdue thee, thou Captain of men!

1770   "For example I myself during fifty years ruled
"beneath the welkin over the jewelled Danes, and I
"by valour made them secure against many a nation
"throughout this world with spears and swords,
"insomuch that I had no apprehension of any rival
"under the circuit of the sky. When lo! in my
"ancestral seat there came a change over all that ;—
"distress where mirth was before, as soon as Grendel,
"the old adversary, became an inmate of mine ; because
"of that visitation I continually carried great anxiety
"at heart. Thanks therefore be to the Governor, the
"Eternal Captain, for that which I have lived to see,
1780 "that I, the old tribulation past, upon that severed,
"that bloody headpiece, with mine eyes do gaze!

"Go now to settle, share the festive joy, crowned
"with honours of war! Thou and I must have dealings
"together in many many treasures, when to-morrow
"comes."

The Goth was glad of mood ; he moved promptly off,
drawing to settle, as the sapient king ordained him.
Then was again as before, to the gallant warriors, to
1790 the company in hall, fair banquet served afresh.

Night's covering grew dim, dark over the banded
men. Uprose all the seniors :—it was that the gray

haired king, the venerable Scylding, was minded
to draw to his bed. Vastly well did the Goth, the
illustrious warrior, like the thought of repose ; promptly
was he, now weary of adventure, the man of far country,
marshalled forth by the chamberlain, one who with
meet ceremony supplied all the wants of a gentleman,
such things as in that day the lords of the main required
to have.

So the great-hearted hero rested him ;—high in
air loomed the edifice, wide-spanning and gold- 1800
gleaming :—the stranger slept within, until the black
raven announced heaven's glory with a blithe heart.
Then came bright light striding over shadow; fiends
scampered off. The ethelings were ready dight to
fare back to their Leeds ;—the magnanimous visitor
was minded to take ship, for a voyage far away.

Then did the hero bid the son of Ecglaf bear away
Hrunting, bade him take his sword, beloved weapon ;
said his thanks for the loan ; quoth that he counted that 1810
war-mate a good one, war-serviceable ; with his words
did not blame the faulchion's edge ; that was a high-
souled lad !

And when the departing warriors were equipped in
harness, the Etheling honoured by the Danes went up
to the dais, where the other warlike hero was ;—he
greeted Hrothgar.

XXVI.

Beowulf's parting interview with Hrothgar, who is moved to tears.

Beowulf son of Ecgtheow uttered speech :—" Now we
"sea-voyagers wish to say, we who have come from far,

1820 "that we are purposing to go to Hygelac. Here we
"have been well entertained to our satisfaction; thou
"hast been to us very generous. If I therefore may
"by any means upon earth undertake for thy further
"gratification, O Captain of men, labours of war
"beyond what I have yet done, I shall be ready
"promptly. If they bring me word over the circuit of
"the floods that neighbours press thee with alarm as
"whilome thy haters did, I will bring thee a thousand
1830 "thanes, warriors to help thee. I can undertake for
⅄ Hygelac, captain of the Goths, young though he be,
"shepherd of people, that he will forward me by words
"and by works, so that I may do high service to thee,
"and for thy support bring a forest of spears, a mighty
"subsidy, when thou shalt have need of men:—if
"moreover Hrethric, princely child, is in treaty for
"admission at the courts of the Goths, he may there
"find many friends; foreign countries are best visited
"by him who is of high worth in himself."
1840 Hrothgar bespake him in answer, "These con-
"siderate words hath the Allwise Lord put into thy
"mind; never heard I a man so young in life speak
"more to purpose; thou art strong in might and ripe
"in understanding; wise in discourse of speech. I
"count it likely, if it cometh to pass that the spear, the
"grim dispatch of battle, taketh away Hrethel's off-
"spring, if ailing or iron taketh thy chieftain, the
"shepherd of the people, and thou hast thy life, that
1850 "the sea-faring Goths have not any thy better to choose
"for king, for treasurer of warriors, if thou art willing
"to hold the realm of thy kinsfolk. To me thy disposi-
"tion is well-liking more and more, beloved Beowulf;

"thou hast achieved, that the nations—Gothic leeds and
"spear-bearing Danes—shall have mutual friendship,
"and strife shall cease, the hostile surprises whence
"they suffered erewhile;—there shall be, while I rule the
"wide realm, a community of treasure : many friends 1860
"shall greet one another with gifts across the bath of
"the gannet ; the ringèd ship shall bring over ocean
"presents and tokens of love. I know the people to
"be equally as towards foe so towards friend constant
"in mind, either way irreproachable, in olden wise."

Then did the Shelter of warriors, the son of Halfdene,
further give into his possession twelve hoarded jewels ;
he bade him go with the presents visit his own people
in comfort, and soon come back again. Then did the 1870
king of noble ancestry, the chief of the Scyldings, kiss
the incomparable thane and clasp him by the neck ; tears
from him fell, the greyhaired man ; forecast was both
ways to the man of old experience, but one way stronger
than the other, namely, that they might never meet
again, proud men in the assembly. To him the man
was so dear, that he could not restrain the passion of
his breast, but deep in the affections of his soul a
secret longing after the beloved man stemmed the
current of his blood.   1880

Beowulf departing thence, a warrior gold-bedight,
trod the grassy earth conscious of wealth :—the sea-
goer, which was riding at anchor, awaited his owner
and lord. Then upon the march was the liberality
of Hrothgar often praised ; that was a king, every
way without reproach ; until old age had bereft him
of the vantage of his prowess,---him who had often
been a terror to many.

XXVII.

The warden of the port, his respectful demeanour. How Beowulf recompensed the care of the boat-warden. The home-bound voyage. Beowulf's progress to Hygelac's mansion. Talk by the way :—the domestic felicity of that young king : his consort Hygd very different from Thrytho. Offa and his son Eomær.

So the troop of gallant bachelors came to the water ;
1890 they wore ring-armour, netted limb-sarks.   The land-
warden observed the return-march of the eorlas, just as
he had done before ;—not with suspicion from the peak
of the cliff did he greet the visitors, but he rode
towards them ; he said to the Leeds of the Wederas
that the bright-mailed explorers came welcome to their
ships.   Then was on the beach the roomy sea-boat
laden with war-harness, the ring-prowed ship with
horses and treasures ; the mast rose high over wealth
from Hrothgar's hoard.
1900   He to the boat-warden presented a gold-bound sword,
insomuch that ever after he was on the mead-bench the
more worshipful by reason of that decoration, that
sword of pedigree.
[The Gothic captain with his band of warriors] betook
him to ship, ploughing deep water ; the Danes' land he
quitted.   Then was by the mast a manner of sea-
garment, a sail with sheet made fast ; the sea-timber
hummed.   There did the wind over the billows not
baffle the wave-floater of her course ; the sea-goer
marched, scudded with foamy throat forward over
1910 the swell, with gorgeous prow over the briny currents,

till they were able to espy the Gothic cliffs, familiar headlands. The keel grated up ashore, with way on her from the wind; she stood on land. Quickly was the hythe-warden ready at the strand, he who already for a long time expectant at the water's edge had eyed the craft of the beloved men; he bound to the shore the wide-bosomed ship with anchor-cables fast, lest the violence of the waves might snatch the winsome craft away from them. Then did he give orders to 1920 carry ashore the princely riches, jewels and wrought gold; not far thence had he to go to find the dispenser of wealth;—" Hygelac the son of Hréthel dwelleth "there at court, himself with his peers, nigh unto the "sea-wall;"—the building was magnifical, the king was majestical, high in his hall; Hygd was very young, wise, of good discretion, though she had experienced few winters in the castle, the daughter of Hæreth; she was howsoever not mean-spirited, nor too grudging of 1930 gifts, of stored possessions, to the Leeds of the Goths.

Thrytho displayed a moody pride, the haughty queen of the people, terrible savagery; no brave man durst venture on that, no one of favourite courtiers, save her own consort, that he openly gazed at her with his eyes; but he might reckon on bands of destruction being prepared for him, woven by hand; in quick succession after arrest was the knife engaged, that the instrument of outrage might settle it, making assassina- 1940 tion famous. Such is not a queenly guise, for a lady to practise, although she be peerless; that a peace-weaver should, upon a false pretence of injury, assail the life of a liege man. However, that was checked by the kinsman of Heming:—those who drink at the ale told an altered story, namely, that she did less of leed-quelling, of personal revenges, from the moment when she was given gold-adorned to the young champion, the noble and the brave; as soon as she had by 1950 her father's counsel voyaged over the fallow flood to seek Offa's hall; there, ever since, she had, as long as she lived in her royal state, been famed for kindness, and had well used life's opportunities; had held high love to the commander of men, who was of all mankind, my story tells, the most excellent between the seas the wide world over; forasmuch as Offa was, the spear-keen man, for graces and war-feats widely celebrated; 1960 with wisdom he ruled his ancestral home; whence Eomær was born for people's aid, kinsman of Heming, grandson of Garmund, and a skilful campaigner.

XXVIII.

The meeting of Beowulf and Hygelac. Hygelac's enquiries. Beowulf's report.

So marched the valiant man, with his band of comrades; he went along the strand treading the sea-laved floor, the spacious foreshores. The world's candle shone, the sun in his course shone from the South; —they pursued their journey, with mighty pace they covered the ground, to where report said that the Shelter of warriors, the banesman of Ongentheow, the war-king young and brave, was in his towers distributing 1970 rings.

Beowulf's arrival was promptly announced to Hygelac, how that there in the precincts the Shelter of fighters, his shield-companion, was coming alive, sound from battle-play, and marching to court. Quickly was cleared, as the ruler commanded, for the travellers, the interior of the hall.

He sate then by the king himself, he who had escaped the struggle, kinsman by kinsman, soon as his liege lord with loud accost had greeted his loyal man with generous 1980 words.   With bombards of mead moved about that hall Hæreth's daughter; she loved the folk, she bore the soothing bowl to the hands of the warriors.

Then began Hygelac graciously to question his bench-fellow in that lofty hall—curiosity urged him—what were the adventures of the Goths at sea :—" How befell "you on your voyage, beloved Beowulf, when thou "suddenly resolvedst to seek combat far away over "salt water, battle at Heorot ?   But didst thou for 1990 "Hrothgar, for the mighty suzerain, at all mend the "wide-known woe ?   I seethed with anxiety therefor, "with gushings of sorrow ; I mistrusted the adventure "for a man so dear ; I long besought thee, that thou "wouldest have no dealings with the destructive mon-"ster, that thou wouldst let the Southron Danes "themselves dispose their quarrel with Grendel.   To "God I offer thanks, for that I have been permitted to "behold thee safe and sound."

Then did Beowulf son of Ecgtheow utter speech ; "That is no secret, Hygelac my liege, the grand meet- 2000 "ing (is known) to numbers of men, what manner of "tournament I and Grendel had upon that field, where "he many a time had wrought sorrow for the conquer-"ing Scyldings, desperate ignominy ;—I avenged it all, "so that not any kin of Grendel upon earth hath cause "to brag of that twilight crash, not he of the detested "race that longest liveth among the fens.

K

2010   "At my first arrival there, I went to the ring-hall to
"greet Hrothgar; promptly did the mighty successor
"of Healfdene, when he knew my purpose, assign me a
"settle by the side of his own son. The company was
"joyous;—never in my life did I see under heaven's
"vault guests in hall more social over mead. At one
"time the lofty queen, bond of peace to the nations,
"passed down the length of the hall, kept the young
"lads to their duty;—often would she bestow on some
"guest a wreathen decoration before she went to settle.
2020 "At another time before the seniors did Hrothgar's
"daughter bear the ale-flagon from end to end of
"the nobles; her I heard the hall-guests name
"Freaware, while she presented to the heroes the
"silver-studded vessel; she, the young, the gold-dight,
"was promised to the gay son of Froda; so hath it
"pleased the Friend of the Scyldings, that he through
"that woman should compose great contentions, san-
"guinary feuds. Often and not seldom anywhere,
2030 "after Leed-slaughter, it is but a little while the
"baneful spear reposes, good though the bride may
"be!"

[XXIX.]

      *   *   *   *   *   *   *   *   *

      *   *   *   *   *   *   *   *   *

[XXX.[1]]

Continuation of Beowulf's Report to Hygelac.

*   *   *   *   *   *   *   *   *

*   *   *   *   "Well may it mislike the ruler of the
"Heathobards and every thane of that nobility, when
"he with the lady goeth into Hall, a prince of the
"Danes amidst the high company; upon him do
"glisten heirlooms of their ancestors, hard and ringèd
"harness, (once) Heathobardic treasure, so long as they
"could retain the mastery of those weapons, until they
"in an unlucky hour led to that buckler-play their dear 2040
"comrades, and their own lives.   Then saith one at the
"beer, one who observes them both, an old lance-
"fighter, one who fully remembers the spear-quelling
"of the men—bitter is the spirit within him;—sore .
"at heart he beginneth to practise upon a young
"champion's feelings through the passions of his
"breast, to awaken war-fury; and that word he
"saith :—

'Canst thou, my friend, recognize the blade, the
'precious steel, which thy father carried into battle, 2050

[1] Neither XXIX nor XXX are marked in the manuscript, and how
Thorpe interpreted these appearances may be seen by his note which
I append :—"Here a part of the MS. is wanting, consisting of the
"remainder of Canto XXVIII, the whole of XXIX, and the beginning
"of XXX." The absence of the Head-Numbers XXIX and XXX, together with the present unsatisfactory commencement of XXX, seem to
justify two-thirds of this statement; but it is not so clear why any of
XXVIII should be thought missing.   Perhaps it may be easier to
imagine a scribe blundering from the midst of one solid paragraph into
another, rather than that he should err at the end of a Canto, which is a
Station that fixes the attention.   But against Thorpe's view is the fact
that the story does not seem correspondingly advanced.

'wearing his helmet for the last time where the Danes
'slew him,—when the indemnity fell through after the
'carnage of men,—and the masters of the battle-field
'were the fiery Scyldings ?   Now here a boy of one or
' other of those banesmen, proud of the spoils, walketh
'our hall, boasteth of the slaughter, and he weareth the
'treasure, of which thou by right shouldst be the
'master !'

   "So urges he and eggs him on at every turn with
"galling words, until the moment comes, that for his
2060 "father's deeds the lady's thane sleepeth blood-spat-
"tered after the falchion's bite, life-doomed ;—the other
"gets him thence away alive ; knows his way well
"enough over land. By and bye the sworn oaths of
"the warriors on either side will be broken ; when
"in Ingeld's mind rankle warlike purposes, and his
"domestic affections grow cooler amidst agitations of
"care. Therefore I esteem not the loyalty of the
"Heathobards, nor the matter of the high alliance
"towards the Danes sincere, the friendship firm./
2070   "I must resume and tell about Grendel again, that
"thou mayest fully know, O wealth-distributor, how far
"was carried the grapple of combatants. After that
"heaven's jewel had passed over the lands away, the
"monster came in fury, grisly with nocturnal ravin,
"to visit us, where we in good heart were guarding
"the hall ;—there was the battle fatal to Hondscio,
"life-bale to the death-doomed ; he was the first to fall,
"a belted champion ; Grendel killed him, my brave
2080 "cousin and thane, with his jaw ; the beloved man's
"body he entirely devoured.

   "But for all that, none the readier was he to depart

"from that gold-hall empty-handed, the bloody-toothed
"assassin of murderous mind ; but confident in strength
"he made trial of me, grasped with ready hand.   The
"glove hanged, huge, and of foul aspect, strengthened
"with intricate bands, it was mysteriously geared with
"devilish machinations and dragon's fells ; therein was
"he minded to have put inoffensive me—the ferocious 2090
"ruffian—with many others; he could not so manage it,
"when I in rage had stood upright.   Too long it is to
"relate, how I repaid the leed-queller for every evil re-
"quital due ;—there did I, my prince, honour thy leeds
"by my works.   He escaped and got away; little while
"did he enjoy the delights of life ;—at any rate, his
"right hand remained behind in Heorot as a mark
"of his track, and he in abject plight, in woeful mood,
"tottered from that place down to the bottom of the 2100
"mere.

    "The Friend of the Scyldings largely rewarded
"me for that encounter with beaten gold and many
"treasures, when the morrow had come and we had
"taken our seats at the banquet.   There was song and
"glee; the venerable Scylding, a large enquirer, told
"tales of long ago ; now a gallant warrior would waken
"the charm of the harp, striking the game-wood ; now
"would one tell a tale true and piteous ; now a strange
"story circumstantially related by the magnanimous 2110
"king.   At another time by and bye one in the fetters
"of eld, an aged veteran, would begin regretting the
"time of youth, of vigour for battle ; his breast within
"him swelled, as the old man revived many memories.
"So we there in that place the live-long day took our
"delight, until that another night arrived to men.

" Eftsoon there was one eager for vengeance, Gren-
" del's mother ; she journeyed woeful ; her son by
2120 " death was taken off, by the hostility of the Wederas.
" The awful mere-wife revenged her bairn, quelled a
" baron furiously ; there was Æschere, the experi-
" enced councillor, bereaved of life ; nothing could they
" do for him when morning came ; the Danish people
" could not consume the lifeless man with fire, could
" not lay the beloved man on the funeral pile ; she had
" borne away the body in fiendish clutches, under the
" mountain waterfall. Of those griefs, which had long
2130 " harassed the sovereign, that was the bitterest to
" Hrothgar. Then did the chieftain in despairing
" mood entreat me—with thy leave—that I in the rush
" of waters would exert valour, hazard life, achieve
" renown ; he promised me meed. I then, as it is
" widely known, found the grim and grisly keeper of
" the whirl-pool's abyss. There we two for a while had
" equal battle. The water gurgled with blood, and I
" in that abysmal dwelling shore off the head of
2140 " Grendel's mother with sword of might ; not easily
" came I thence away with my life ; I was not then
" fated to die as yet, but upon me did the Shelter of
" heroes, the son of Healfdene, gratefully bestow foison
" of treasures.

XXXI.

**Beowulf concludes his report ; and then he renders up
to Hygelac, and to the queen, his gifts and rewards.
Beowulf is promoted. Ultimately he reigned.**

" So the imperial king lived in good customs ;--by no
" means had I missed the rewards, the meed of my

"achievement, but he gave me precious things, did
"Healfdene's son, into my own disposal; them will I
"render unto thee, noble king, as a grateful presenta-
"tion.   Surely all my satisfactions are along of thee; 2150
"I have hardly any kinsman in chief, save thee,
"O Hygelac."

Then he ordered to bring in a boar head-crest, a
battle-towering helmet, a gray mail-coat, a gallant
cutlass; and he thereafter descanted :—"This battle-
"suit did Hrothgar, sapient prince, give to me, and with
"express word he bade, that I the pedigree thereof
"should report to thee;—he said that king Hiorogâr,
"lord of the Scyldings, had it for a long while; nathless
"he would not give to his own son, the keen Heoro- 2160
"ward, though he was loyal to him, this breast-apparel.
"Enjoy all well !"

I heard that upon those ornaments four horses,
exactly alike, followed close, apple-fallow; he to him
made grateful presentation of horses and of treasures.
So should a kinsman do, and not by any means spread
the deceitful net for his fellow, with hidden artifice
contrive death for a comrade.   To Hygelac, bold in
battle, his nephew was throughly loyal, and either to 2170
other studious of kindnesses.

I heard that he presented the carcanet to Hygd,
the curiously wrought wonderful jewel, the one that
Wealhtheow, daughter of a prince, had given to him;
and therewithal three palfreys elegant and saddle-dight;
—from that time was her breast decorated upon collar-
bestowing occasions.

So Ecgtheow's son increased in confidence, a man
known in wars, in valiant deeds; he conducted him-

self with discretion; never did he smite his hearth-
2180 fellows in their cups; his was no ruffian soul, but he of
all mankind most prudently controlled the mighty talent
that God had given him, like a brave soldier. Little
esteemed he had been for a long time, as the children
of the Goths had not counted him good for anything,
nor had the Captain of hosts been pleased to make him
of much dignity at the mead-bench; very often they said
that he was slack, an unpromising prince;—reversal of
every indignity came to the man when he was radiant
with glory.

2190   Then commanded the Shelter of warriors, the battle-
famed king, to fetch-in Hrethel's heir-loom, mounted
with gold;—there was not among the Goths at that
time a treasure of more distinction in the way of a
sword;—that he laid upon Beowulf's bosom, and
conferred upon him seven thousands, mansion,
and seat of authority.

Both of them alike possessed in that community
hereditary land, a family estate; but the empery was
rather to the other, who in that respect had the pre-
2200 eminence. By and bye that accrued, in process of
days, through violence of war, when Hygelac had fallen,
and instruments of war despite shield and buckler had
proved fatal to Heardred; what time the tough war-
wolves, the bellicose Scylfings, had come to look him
in the face among his battalions, and had humbled
from his raids the nephew of Hereric.

Consequently the broad realm came to the hand of
Beowulf; he governed well fifty winters—that was
2210 a venerable king, an old êthel-warden—until one
began in dark nights, even a dragon, to have mastery;

one that on a high heath kept a hoard, a steep stone-
castle; a path lay beneath, unfrequented by people.
Therewithin had gone some man or other, [deftly] he
took of the heathen hoard, [took a thing] glistening
with precious metal;—that he afterwards [rued], that
he had tricked the horrid keeper while sleeping, with
thievish dexterity.................that he was 2220
infuriate.

THE THIRD PART.

XXXII.

**How it happened that the man robbed the Dragon's
hoard.   That treasure was the accumulated store of
ancient and forgotten warriors.   The Dragon prepares
revenge.   The beginning of the fatal war.**

Not of set purpose nor by his own free choice had
he visited the dragon's hoard, he who brought sore
trouble on himself; but for dire necessity had he, the
slave of some one or other of the sons of men, fled
from outrageous stripes a houseless wretch, and into
that place had blundered like a man in guilty terror.
[*Here four (or five) mutilated lines seem to say that the
fugitive, though quickly horror-struck at his new danger,
still by the impetus of despair borne forward had espied* 2230
a cup of precious metal.]   There was a quantity of such
things in that earth-cavern, ancient acquisitions; just
as some unknown man in days of yore had in pensive
thought hidden them there, the prodigious legacy of
a noble race, treasures of worth.   Death had carried

them all off previously, and that solitary one then of
the proud company who had there longest kept afoot,
a possessor mourning lost friends, would fain survive,
2240 if only that he might for a little space enjoy the long-
accumulated wealth.

A barrow already existed on the down, nigh by the
waves, sheer over the cliff, cunningly secured; therein
did the owner of rings carry a ponderous quantity of
beaten gold: a few words he spake: "Hold thou
"now O earth, now that the heroes could not, the
"possessions of mighty men. Lo! in thee at first the
"brave men found it; a violent death carried them
2250 "away, a fearful slaughter carried off every one of
"the men, my peers, who surrendered this life; they
"attained the joy of the (supernal) hall. Not one have
"I to wear a sword, or furbish the bossy tankard, the
"precious drink-stoup; the valiant are departed other-
"where. Now must the hard helmet, damascened with
"gold, shed its intaylèd foliations; the furbishers sleep,
"they whose task it was to keep the masks of war;
"likewise the war-coat which in battle and through the
"crash of shields was proof against the bite of swords,
2260 "shall moulder like the warrior. No longer can the
"ringèd mail along with the war-chief widely travel by
"the hero's side;—no delight of harp, no joy of glee-
"wood, no good hawk swinging through the hall, no
"swift horse tramping in the castle-court. Destructive
"death hath sent many generations far away." Thus
did he with sorrowful heart lament his unhappiness,
sole survivor of all he sadly wept, by day and by night,
2270 until that death's ripple touched at his heart.

The dazzling hoard was found open standing by the old

pest of twilight, the flaming one that haunteth barrows, the scaly spiteful dragon, that flyeth by night, surrounded with fire, whom country-folk hold in awful dread. His portion is to resort to the hoard under ground, where he with winters aged shall guard heathen gold ; he will be no whit the better for it. So had that wide-ravager for three hundred winters held in the earth an enormous treasure-house, until that one angered him, 2280 a man angered his mood ;—to his chieftain the man bore a tankard bossed with gold, and prayed his lord for a covenant of peace. Then was the hoard rifled, quantity of jewels carried off; the friendless man had his petition granted. The lord contemplated men's ancient work for the first time.

When the Worm woke, the quarrel was begun ; forthwith he sniffed the scent along the rock ; the marble-hearted one found the enemy's track ;—he had stepped forth abroad with undetected craft, hard 2290 by the dragon's head. So may that man, who retains the fealty of the Supreme, elude death and freely escape both harm and pursuit. The hoard-keeper sought diligently over the ground, he wanted to find the man, the man who had wrought him mischief in his sleep ; fiery and in raging mood he often swung around the tumulus, all out round about; there was not any man there in that desert waste. Nevertheless he exulted in purpose of battle, of bloody work ; at intervals he would dash back into the barrow, would seek the costly vessel ; presently he had satisfied him- 2300 self of that, that some one of manfolk had invaded the gold, the mighty treasures. The hoard-keeper waited with difficulty until evening came ; so enraged

was the master of the barrow, the malignant one designed with fire to revenge the loss of the precious tankard. Presently the day was gone, the Worm had his will; no longer would he bide in fencèd wall, but he issued forth with burning, equipped with fire. The
2310 commencement of it was frightful to the people in the country, likewise it speedily had a sore ending upon their Benefactor.

XXXIII.

The Dragon's devastations. The King's mansion burnt. Beowulf's proud resolve to fight the dragon single handed. Retrospect of the hero's former achievements, and how he had become king.

Then the monster began to spirt fire-gleeds, to burn the cheerful farmsteads; the flame-light glared aloft, in defiance of men; the hostile air-flyer would leave nothing there alive. The war-craft of the Worm was manifest in all parts; the rage of the deadly foe was seen far and near; how the ravaging invader hated and ruined the Gothic people; to his hoard he shot
2320 back again, to his dark mansion, before the hour of day. He had encompassed the landfolk with flame, with fire and conflagration; he trusted in his mountain, his war-craft, and his rampart; that confidence deceived him.

Then was the crushing news reported to Beowulf with swiftness and certainty, that his own mansion, best of buildings, was melting away in fiery eddies, even the gift-seat of the Goths. That was to the goodman a rude experience in his breast, hugest of heart-griefs; the wise man felt as if he should, in despite of venerable law, break out against Providence, 2330 against the Eternal Lord, with bitter outrage ; his breast within him surged with murky thoughts, in a manner unwonted with him. The fire-drake had desolated the stronghold of the nobles, the sea-board front, that enclosèd pale, with fiery missiles. For him therefore the war-king, the lord of the Storm-folk, studied revenge. He gave orders, that they should make for him, the shelter of warriors, the captain of knights, wholly of iron, a war-shield, a master-piece ; he knew assuredly, that forest-timber would not serve 2340 him, linden-wood against flame ! Destined he was, the prince of proved valour, to meet the end of his allotted days, of his worldly life ;—and the Worm (was to die) at the same time, long though he had held the hoarded wealth.

Then did he, of rings the patron, think it scorn that he should go seek the wide-flyer with a band, with a large host ; he had no fear of the encounter for himself, nor did the Worm's war-craft at all subdue his puissance and enterprize ; forasmuch as he whilere, in shrewd jeopardy, had carried him safe through many 2350 a contest, many a battle-crash, since the time that he, a victorious boy, had purged Hrothgar's hall, and with battailous grip had done for Grendel's kinsfolk, a loath-some brood.

Not by any means littlest of hand-to-hand encounters was that, where Hygelac was slain, what time the Gothic king in the clash of battle, the liege-lord of nations, in the Frieslands, the son of Hrethel, died by the thirsty sword, felled with bill. Thence Beowulf came off by his own peculiar strength, he went through a labour 2360

of swimming; he had upon his arm thirty sets of war-
harness when he all alone went down into the deep.
The Hetware, who had confronted him bearing the
linden, had no cause to be jubilant over the affray;
few arrived back again from that battle-wolf to visit
their home. He overswam the circuit of the fore-
shore waters, Ecgtheow's son, woe-begone and solitary,
and got back to his people, where Hygd proffered
2370 him treasure and realm, jewels and royal throne;—she
had not confidence in the Child, that he against
foreigners would be able to vindicate the ancestral
seats, now that Hygelac was dead. None the more
readily could the bereaved people prevail with the
Ætheling on any conditions whatever, that he should
become Heardred's lord, or should consent to accept
the kingdom; nevertheless he held to him in the
public assembly with friendly guidance, respectfully
with honour, up to the time that he became of full age
and reigned over the Storm-Goths.

2380   He (Heardred) was visited from over sea by out-
lawed companions, Ohthere's sons; they had renounced
allegiance to the crowned head of the Scylfings, the
most excellent of the sea-kings that dispensed bounty in
the Swedish realm, illustrious potentate. That was the
limit of his (Heardred's) career; he there for his hospitality got a deadly wound with dynt of sword, did
Hygelac's son; and Ongentheow's (grand)son returned
to draw to his home, when Heardred had fallen; he
2390 let Beowulf possess the royal throne and reign over
the Goths;—that was a good king.

XXXIV.

When Beowulf had come to the throne by the king's death he had remembered Heardred's banesman with vengeance. Preparing now for his last battle, he is filled with retrospective thoughts, and reviews his life from childhood.

For that national disaster he meditated retribution in later days ; he became a friend to Eadgils in his desolation. With force of men he supported the son of Ohthere over the wide sea, with warriors and weapons ; he had his revenge at length by means of cold and painful marches ; he deprived the king of life.

Thus had he, Ecgtheow's son, come well off out of all his contests, his perilous encounters, his daring adventures, up to that particular day when he had to 2400 engage with the Dragon.   So he went twelfsome forth, he the Goths' commander, enflamed with fury, to reconnoitre the Dragon.   He had by that time learnt what was the origin of the feud, the quarrel baleful to men ; into his lap the precious vase magnificent had come by the informant's hand.   That was the thirteenth man in the party, he who had set up the quarrel at first ; captive, rueful, he was compelled submissively to shew the way to the spot ; he went against his will, to where 2410 he knew of a lonely earthen dome, a tumulus roofed with mould, near the sea-breakers, the clash of billows ; it was inwardly full of curiosities and filagrees ; the portentous keeper, aggressive war-demon, defended the golden treasures, old subterranean inhabitant ; no easy bargain to go in for was that, be the man who he may.   Then did the resolute king sit him down on the

headland, and from that point he bade farewell, the
Gothic lord, to his hearth-fellows;—he had a sorrowful
2420 soul, agitated and boding, Wyrd awfully nigh, which
was to greet the aged man, visit the soul's recess, divide
asunder life from body; not long then was the Ætheling's soul encircled with flesh.

Beowulf, Ecgtheow's son, uttered speech: "Many a
"foughten broil have I lived through in my youth,
"many an hour of contest; all that I now remember.
"I was seven winter old when the master of riches, the
"liege-lord of peoples, received me from my father;
2430 "king Hrethel held me as his own, gave me pocket-
"money and sustenance, remembered kinship; I was not
"at all less pleasing to him as a varlet in the castle, than
"any one of his own boys, Herebeald and Hæthcyn, or
"my own lord Hygelac. For the eldest a bloody bed
"was unnaturally strown by the doings of a brother,
"inasmuch as Hæthcyn by arrow from horn-bow brought
"him down, his high kinsman; he missed the target and
2440 "shot his brother; one brother killed the other with
"bloody dart; that was an assault past compensation,
"dastardly perpetrated, heart-paralyzing;—any way
"and every way it was unavoidable that the etheling
"must quit life unavenged.

"In like manner it is a rueful thing for an aged
"husbandman to experience, that his son should ride
"young on the gallow-tree, and he wail a dirge, a
"sorrowful song, while his son hangs for the raven's
"benefit, and he, old and of ripe experience, cannot
2450 "bring him any help. Continually he is reminded,
"every morning, of his son's absence; he cares not to
"look forward to another heir in the family seat, when

" the one hath through violent death received for his " deeds.

" Sorrow-worn he beholds in his son's bower a " deserted guest-hall, a lodging for the wind, bereft of " hilarity ; the riders sleep, the men are in the grave ; " there is no sound of harp, no revels in the courts, as " there were once.

XXXV.

Beowulf continues the story of Hrethel, who died of a broken heart. Further discourses of Beowulf. He gives a great shout, and the Dragon comes forth. The fight begins ; Beowulf in distress.

" He takes to his bed ; chanteth a lay of sorrow, 2460 " the solitary one in memory of one (departed) ; to him " all seemed too open, both country and town-place.

" So did the crownèd head of the Storm-folk, in " memory of Herebeald, carry about a tumult of heart- " sorrow ; he could not possibly requite the feud upon " the man-slayer ; neverthemore could he pursue the " warrior with hostile deeds, though he was not " beloved by him. He then with the sorrow, where- " with that wound had stricken him, resigned the en- " joyment of human life, chose the light of God ; to his 2470 " children he left, as a wealthy man doth, land and " castle, when he went out of life.

" Then was there provocation and reprisal between " Swedes and Goths over wide water, claims reciprocal, " obstinate hard struggle, after Hrethel was dead, and " Ongentheow's sons were impetuous, keen for adven- " ture, and would not keep peace across the lakes ; but " about Hreosnabeorh they often contrived a truculent " ambuscade. That did my cousins (i. e. Hæthcyn

2480 "and Hygelac) revenge, the outrage and the wrong, as
"it was notorious, though one of them paid for it with
"his life, a hard bargain :—to Hæthcyn, the Gothic
"monarch, the war was fatal. Then in the morning,
"so runs the tale, brother avenged brother with sharp
"sword upon the smiter, where Ongentheow engaged
"with Eofor ; the war-helmet was split, the aged Scyl-
"fing fell blanched in death ; the smiting hand made
"reckoning for feuds enough, shrank not from the
"deadly swoop.

2490 "The treasures which he had bestowed upon
"me I paid him in war, as opportunity was given me,
"with flashing sword ; he gave me land, a dwelling-
"place, the joy of proprietorship. No need had
"he, that he among the Gepidæ, or the Spear-Danes,
"or in the Swedish realm, should have to seek inferior
"champions, hire them with pay ; ever would I be
"to the fore in his marching ranks, single in the
"van ; and so shall I lifelong practise warfare, while
2500 "this sword holdeth out, which hath often done me
"good service early and late, since the time when of
"my prowess I did with (unarmed) hand kill Dæghrefn,
"the champion of the Hugas ; he might not (as he
"had expected) bring the rich spoils (viz. of the slain
"Hygelac ?), the breast-decoration, to the Frisian king ;
"but in the battle-field he crouched, the standard-
"keeper, prince in chivalry. No weapon was his
"bane, but the war-grapple checked his heart-currents,
"broke his bone-house. Now (on the contrary) must
"the weapon's edge, the hand and the hard sword,
"contend for the treasure."

2510 Beowulf uttered speech, with boastful words he

spake, for the last time: "I hazarded many wars in "youth; yet again will I, the aged keeper of the folk, "seek strife, and do famously; if the fell ravager out of "his earthen dome will come forth to meet me." Then did he address a word of greeting to each of his men, the keen helm-wearers, for the last time, his own familiar comrades. "I would not bear sword or weapon to "meet the Worm, if I knew how I might otherwise "maintain my vaunt against the monster, as I formerly 2520 "did against Grendel. But there I expect fire deadly "scorching, blast and venom; for that reason I "have upon me shield and byrnie. I will not flee "away from the keeper of the mountain, no not a foot "space; but it shall be decided between us two on this "rampart, as Wyrd allots us, (and) the Governor of every "man. I am in spirit so eager for action, that I cut "short bragging against the wingy warrior. Await ye "on the mountain, with your byrnies about you, men- 2530 "at-arms, to see which of us twain may after deadly "tussle best be able to survive his hurt. That is not "your mission, nor any man's task save mine alone, "that he try strength against the monster, achieve "heroism. I must with daring conquer gold, or else "war carrieth, pitiless life-bale carrieth away your "lord!"

Up rose then by the brink the resolute warrior, stern under his helmet, he wore battle-sark among rugged 2540 cliffs, he trusted the strength of his single manhood; such is not the way of a craven. Then he beheld near the rampart—he who, excellent in accomplishments, had survived a great number of wars, of battle-clashes, when armed men close—beheld where stood a rocky arch, and out of it a stream breaking from the barrow, the surface of that burne was steaming hot with cruel fire; nigh to the hoard could not the hero unscorched any while survive for the flame of the dragon.

2550 Then did the prince of the Storm-Goths, being elate with rage, let forth word out of his breast, the strong-hearted stormed; the shout penetrated within (the cavern), vibrating clear as a battle-cry, under the hoary rock. Fury was stirred; the hoard-warder recognized speech of man; opportunity was there no more, to stickle for terms of peace. In advance first of all there came the recking breath of the monster, out from the rock, a hot jet of defiance; the 2560 ground trembled. The warrior under the barrow side, the Gothic captain, swung his mighty shield against the hideous customer; therewithal was the heart of the ringy worm incited to seek battle. Already the brave war-king had drawn sword, ancient heirloom of speedy edge; each of the belligerents had a dread of the other. Resolute in mind the Prince of friends took stand well up to his hoised shield, while the Worm buckled suddenly in a bow;—he stood to his weapons.

2570 Then did the flaming foe, curved like an arch, advance upon him with headlong shuffle. The shield effectually protected life and limb a less while for the glorious chieftain than his sanguine hope expected, supposing he, that-time, early in the morning, was to achieve glory in the strife;—so had Wyrd not ordained it. Up swung he his hand, the Gothic captain, he smote the spotted horror with the mighty heirloom, that its brown edge turned upon the bony crust; less effectually bit than was required by the

king's need, who was sorely pressed.   Then was the 2580
keeper of the barrow after that shrewd assault furious
with rage, cast forth devouring fire, the deadly sparks
sprang every way : the gold-friend of the Goths plumed
him not on strokes of vantage ; the war-bill had failed
him with its bared edge on the foe, as it had not been
expected to do, metal of old renown.   That was no
light experience, inducing the mighty son of Ecgtheow
to relinquish t h a t emprize ; he must consent to
inhabit a dwelling otherwhere ;—so must every man 2590
resign allotted days.

Then was it not long until the combatants closed
again.   The hoard-warder rallied his courage, out of
his breast shot steam, as beginning again ;—direly
suffering, encompassed with fire, was he who erewhile
had ruled men.   Not (alas!) in a band did his life-
guardsmen, sons of ethelings, stand about him with
war-custom of comrades ; no, to the wood they slunk,
to shelter life.   In one only of them did his soul surge 2600
in a tumult of grief ;—kindred may never be diverted
from duty, for the man who is rightly minded.

XXXVI.

Beowulf had one faithful follower in the desperate struggle. His fatal wound.

Wiglaf was his name, Weohstan's son, a beloved
warrior, a Leed of the Scylfings, a kinsman of Ælfhere :
he beheld his liege-lord under helmet, distressed by the
heat.   Then did he remember the (territorial) Honour
which he (Beowulf) had formerly given him, the well-
stocked homestead of the Wægmundings, every poli-

tical prerogative which his father had enjoyed; then
2610 could he not refrain; hand grasped shield, yellow linden,
drew the old sword, known among men as the relic of
Eánmund, son of Ohthere, whom, when a lordless exile,
Weohstan had slain, in fair fight, with weapon's edge;
and from his kindred had carried off the brown-mottled
helmet, ringèd byrnie, old mysterious sword; which
Onela yielded to him, his nephew's war-harness, ac-
coutrement complete; not a word spake he (Onela)
about the feud, although he (Weohstan) had killed his
2620 brother's son. He (Weohstan) retained the spoils
many years, bill and byrnie, until when his boy was
able to claim warrior's rank, like his father before him;
then gave he to him before the Goths armour untold of
every sort; after which he departed out of life, ripe for
the parting journey.

Now this was the first adventure for the young
champion wherein he had with his liege lord to enterprize the risk of war; his courage did not melt in
him, nor did his kinsman's heirloom prove weak in the
conflict; a fact which the Worm experienced, as soon
2630 as they had come to close quarters.

Wiglaf discoursed much that was fitting; he said to his
comrades that his soul was sad :—"I recall the time,
"when we enjoyed the mead, then did we promise our
"lord in the festive hall, to him who gave us rings, that
"we would repay him the war-harness, if any need of
"this kind should befall him, would repay him for
"helmets and tempered swords. That is why he chose
2640 "us of his host for this adventure by his own preference,
"reminded us of glory and promised rewards, because
"he counted us brave warriors, keen helm-wearers;

"although our lord had designed single-handed to ac-
"complish this mighty work, the shepherd of his people,
"forasmuch as he of all men had achieved most of famous
"exploits, of desperate deeds.   Now is the day come, that
"our liege lord behoves the strength of brave warriors;
"let us go to him, help our war-chief, while the scorching
"heat is on him, the grim fiery terror ! God knows of 2650
"me, that I had much liever the flame should swallow
"my body with my gold-giver. Me thinketh it indecent,
"that we bear our shields back to our home, unless we
"can first quell the foe, and rescue the life of the Storm-
"folk's ruler.   I know well those were not the old
"habits of service, that he alone of the Gothic nobles
"should bear the brunt, should sink in fight; our
"sovereign must be requited for sword and helm,
"byrnie and stately uniform, and so he shall by me,
"though a common death take us both ¹."   2660

Then he sped through the deadly reek, he came with
helm on head to his lord's assistance ; few words spake
he : "My liege Beowulf, now make good all that which
"thou once saidst in time of youth, that thou never by
"thy life-time wouldest let thy glory decline ; now must
"thou, glorious in deeds, etheling impetuous, with all
"thy might defend life; I shall support thee to the
"utmost."

After these words were spoken, the Worm came on in
fury, the fell malignant monster came on for the second 2670
time, with fire-jets flashing, to engage his enemies, hated
men ; with the waves of flame the shield was consumed
all up to the boss; the mail-coat could not render

¹ Here I have adopted Prof. Sophus Bugge's emendation. See note
below.

assistance to the young warrior; but the young stripling
valorously went forward under his kinsman's shield
when his own was reduced to ashes by the gleeds.
Then once more the warlike king remembered glory,
remembered his forceful strength, so smote with battle-
2680 bill that it stood in the monster's head, desperately impelled. Nægling flew in splinters, Beowulf's sword
betrayed him in battle, though old and monumental
gray. To him was it not granted, that edges of iron
should help him in fight; too strong was the hand of
the man who with his stroke overtaxed (as I have heard
say) all swords whatsoever; so that when he carried to
conflict a weapon preternaturally hard, he was none the
better for it.

Then for the third time was the monstrous ravager,
2690 the infuriated fire-drake, roused to vengeance; he
rushed on the heroic man, as he had yielded ground,
fiery and destructive, his entire neck he enclosed with
lacerating teeth; he was bloodied over with the vital
stream; gore surged forth in waves.

XXXVII.

The Dragon slain. Beowulf in mortal agony.

Then I heard tell how, in the glorious king's extremity, the young noble put forth exemplary prowess
of force and daring, as was his nature to; he regarded
not that (formidable) head, but the valiant man's
hand was scorched, while he helped his kinsman, insomuch that he smote the fell creature a little lower
2700 down, the man-at-arms did, with such effect that the
sword penetrated, the chased and gilded sword, yea

with such effect that the fire began to subside from that moment.

Then once more the beloved king recovered his senses, drew the war-knife, biting and battle-sharp, which he wore on his mail-coat; the crownèd head of the Storm-folk gashed the Worm in the middle. They had quelled the foe, death-daring prowess had executed revenge, and they two together, cousin ethelings, had destroyed him;—such should a fellow be, a thane at need. To the chieftain that was the supreme triumphal hour of his career—by his own 2710 deeds—of his life's completed work.

Then began the wound which the earth-dragon had just now inflicted on him, to inflame and swell. That he soon discovered, that in his breast fatal mischief was working, venom in the inward parts. Then the Etheling went until he sate him on a stone by the mound, thoughtfully pondering; he looked upon the cunning work of dwarfs, how there the world-old earth-dome do contain within it stone arches firmly set upon piers. Upon him then, gory from conflict, illustrious 2720 monarch, the thane immeasureably good, ladled water with hand upon his natural chieftain, battle-worn;— and unloosened his helmet. Beowulf discoursed—in spite of his hurt he spake, his deadly exhausting wound; he knew well that he had spent his hours, his enjoyment of earth; surely all was gone of the tale of his days, death immediately nigh—"Now I would have "given my war-weeds to my son, had it so been that 2730 "any heir had been given to come after me, born of my "body. I have ruled this people fifty winters;—there "was not the king, not any king of those neighbouring

N

"peoples, who dared to greet me with war-mates,
"to menace with terror. I in my habitation observed
"social obligations, I held my own with justice, I
"have not sought insidious quarrels, nor have I sworn
"many false oaths. Considering all this, I am able,
2740 "though sick with deadly wounds, to have comfort;
"forasmuch as the Ruler of men cannot charge me with
"murder-bale of kinsmen, when my life quitteth the body.
    "Now quickly go thou, to examine the treasure,
"under the hoary rock, beloved Wiglaf, now the Worm
"lieth dead, sleepeth sore wounded, of riches bereaved.
"Be now on the alert, that I may ascertain the ancient
"wealth, the golden property, may fully survey the
"brilliant, the curious gems ; that I may be able the
2750 "more contentedly, after (seeing) the treasured store, to
"resign my life, and the lordship which I long have
"held."

XXXVIII.

Beowulf is gratified with seeing the treasures ; he demises the crown, and dies.

Then I heard tell how the son of Wihstan after the
injunction promptly obeyed his wounded death-sick
lord ; bore his ring-mail, linkèd war-sark, under the
roof of the barrow. Then the victorious youth, as he
went along by the stony bench, the true and courageous
thane, beheld many jewels of value, gold glistening, in-
denting the ground, wondrous things in the barrow ;—
2760 and the lair of the Worm, the old dawn-flyer—vases
standing, choice vessels of men of old, with none to
burnish them, their incrustations fallen away. There
was many a helmet, old and rusty, many a bracelet, with

appendage of trinkets. Treasure may easily, gold in the earth, may easily make a fool of any man; heed it who will! Likewise he saw looming above the hoard a banner all golden, greatest marvel of handi-work, woven with arts of incantation; out of it there stood forth a gleam of light, insomuch that he was able to discern the surface of the floor, and survey the 2770 strange curiosities. Of the Worm there was not any appearance, but the knife had put him out of the way.

Then heard I how in the chambered mound the old work of dwarfs was spoiled by a single man, how he gathered into his lap cups and platters at his own discretion; the banner also he took, the most brilliant of ensigns; the sword with its iron edge had even now dispatched the old proprietor, the one who had been the possessor of these treasures for a long while; a hot 2780 and flaming terror he had waged for the hoard, gushing with destruction at midnights; until he died the death.

The messenger was in haste, eager to return, fraught with spoils; painfully he wondered in his brave soul whether he should find alive the prince of the Storm-folk, on the open ground where he left him erst, chivalrously dying. He then bearing the treasures, found the illustrious king, his captain, bleeding from his wounds, at the extremity of life; he began again to 2790 sprinkle him with water, until the point of speech forced open the treasures of his breast. Beowulf discoursed, the old man in pain, he contemplated the gold: "I do "utter a thanksgiving to the Lord of all, to the king of "glory, to the eternal captain, for those spoils upon "which I here do gaze; to think that I have been per-"mitted to acquire such for my Leeds before the day of

2800 "my death. Now I have sold my expiring life-term for
"a hoard of treasure; ye now shall provide for the
"requirements of the Leeds; I cannot be any longer
"here. Order my brave warriors to erect a lofty cairn
"after the bale-fire, at the headland over the sea; it shall
"tower aloft on Hronesness for a memorial to my Leeds,
"that sea-faring men in time to come may call it
"Beowulf's Barrow, those who on distant voyages drive
"their foamy barks over the scowling floods."

The brave-hearted monarch took off from his neck
2810 the golden collar and gave it to the thane, to the young
spear-fighter, his gold-hued helmet, coronet, and byrnie;
bade him brook them well: "Thou art the last remnant
"of our stock, of the Wægmundings; Fate has swept
"all my kinsmen away into eternity, princes in chivalry;
"I must after them."

That was the aged man's latest word, from the medi-
tations of his breast, before he chose the bale-fire, the
hot consuming flames;—out of his bosom the soul
2820 departed, to enter into the lot of the Just.

XXXIX.

A brief review of the situation. Wiglaf upbraids the
recreant gesiðas. He pronounces upon them and their
kin a sentence of degradation.

Thus had a hard experience overtaken the inexpe-
rienced youth, that he saw upon the ground the man
who was dearest to him at his life's end in a helpless
condition. His destroyer likewise lay dead, the horrible
earth-dragon, bereft of life, crushed in ruin; no longer
was the coilèd Worm to be lord of the jewel-treasures,

but they had been wrested from him with weapons of
iron, hard battle-sharp relics of hammers, insomuch that 2830
the wide-flyer tamed by wounds had fallen on earth
nigh to the hoard-chamber; no more through the regions of air did he sportively whirl at midnights, and
elate over his treasured property display his presence;
but on earth he collapsed, through mighty hand of
warrior-prince.

Howbeit, that has rarely in the world prospered
with men, even men of fame,—by my information,—
daring though a man might be in all deeds whatsoever; that he should rush against the breath of the
poisonous destroyer, or with hands molest the ring- 2840
hall, if he found the keeper waking, at home in the
barrow. | Beowulf had purchased the gain of princely
treasures with his death; he had howsoever reached the
end of transitory life.

Then was it not long until the war-laggards quitted
the wood, the faint-hearted traitors, ten all together,
those who whilere durst not sport their lances in the
great need of their liege lord; but they in shame bore 2850
their shields, their war-weeds, to the place where the
aged warrior lay dead;—they looked upon Wiglaf!

He sate wearied out, the active champion, nigh his
lord's shoulder; was refreshing him with water; his
care availed nothing; he could not retain upon earth,
well as he would have wished it, that chieftain's life;
nor turn the Almighty's will; the dispensation of God
would take effect upon men of all conditions, just
as it does at present. Then had the young man 2860
a grim answer promptly ready for such as erst had

failed in courage.   Wiglaf discoursed, Weohstan's son ;
the youth with sorrowful heart looked upon men whom
he no longer loved :—

"That, look you, may a man say, a man who is
"minded to speak the truth, that the chieftain who
"gave you those decorations, military apparel, which
"ye there stand upright in, · when he at ale-bench often
"presented to inmates of his hall helmet and byrnie,
2870 "as a prince to thanes, of such make as he far or near
"could procure most trusty—that he utterly threw away
"those war-weeds miserably.   When stress of battle
"overtook him, the folk-king had by no means cause to
"boast of his companions-in-arms ; nevertheless it was
"accorded to him by God the ordainer of victories, that
"he avenged himself single-handed with his weapon,
"when his valour was put to the proof.   Little protec-
"tion could I afford him in the conflict, and I attempted
"nevertheless what was beyond my ability, to help my
2880 "kinsman ;—ever was he (the dragon) the feebler, when
" I with sword smote the destroyer, the fire less violently
"gushed from his inwards.   Defenders too few pressed
"round their prince, when the dire moment overtook
"him.   Now must (all) sharing of treasure, and presen-
"tation of swords, all patrimonial wealth and estate,
"escheat from your kin ; every man of that family may
"roam destitute of land-right, as soon as ethelings at
"a distance are informed of your desertion, your ig-
2890 "nominious conduct.   Death is preferable, for every
"warrior, rather than a life of infamy."

XL.

**Announcement of the event to the armèd host.   The
envoy adds a discourse, reviewing the situation.**

Orders gave he then to announce the issue of the
conflict to the camp up over the seacliff, where the host
of eorls, from morning all day long, had with anxious
hearts sate by their shields, in divided anticipation
between a fatal day and the return of the beloved man.
Little reticent was he of the latest tidings, he who rode
up the bluff; he truthfully spake out in the hearing
of all: "Now is the bounteous chief of the Leeds of 2900
"the Stormfolk, the captain of the Goths, motionless on
"bed of death, he dwells in war-like repose by the
"deeds of the Worm! with him in even case lieth his
"mortal antagonist, smitten with dirk-wounds :—with
"sword he could not upon the monster by any means
"effect a wound.   Over Beowulf sitteth Wîglâf, Wih-
"stan's boy, a living eorl over a dead ; over his uncon-
"scious head he holdeth guard against friend and foe.   2910
"Now the Leeds may expect a time of war, as soon
"as the king's fall is published abroad among Franks
"and Frisians.   The obstinate quarrel with the Hugas
"was set up when Hygelac came with embarkèd army
"upon the Frisian land, where the Hetware in battle
"vanquished him ; resolutely they struck with over-
"whelming force, insomuch that the mailèd warrior was
"compelled to bow his head ; he fell among the fighting
"men : far was he from giving spoils as chieftain to his 2920
"veterans ;—to us ever since that time has the favour
"of the Merwing been unaccorded.

"Nor do I anywise count upon peace or good under-
"standing on the side of Sweden;—indeed it was a
"far-famed story, how that Ongentheow slew Hæthcyn
"the son of Hrethel by Ravenswood, whenas the warlike
"Scylfings had been the first to invade for sheer
"insolence the people of the Goths.   Promptly did the
"veteran, the father of Ohthere, old and awful, deliver
2930 "his onslaught, demolished the sea-king (Hæthcyn),
"rescued his consort, the aged man rescued the wife of
"his youth, though plundered of her jewels, the mother
"of Onela and of Ohthere, and then pursued his deadly
"foes, until they got away, with great difficulty, into
"Ravensholt, bereaved of their lord.   Then did he, with
"host drawn out, surround those whom the sword had
"left, men exhausted with wounds, he repeatedly
"threatened woe to the poor band all the livelong
2940 "night: he said that in the morning he would reach
"them with the edge of the sword, and (hang) some on
"gallow-trees to please the birds.

"Courage at length returned to the dejected men with
"dawn of day, when they heard Hygelac's horn, and the
"sound of his trumpet; presently the brave (prince)
"came marching upon their track with the best of his
"Leeds.

XLI.

Conclusion of the envoy's discourse.   The battalion visits the scene of the supreme conflict.

"Then was the gory track of Swedes and Goths, the
"deadly strife of men, widely conspicuous, how the folk

"on either side revived the feud. Then did the valiant
"man proceed with his comrades, the solemn veteran, 2950
"to seek a place of strength ; the warrior Ongentheow
"turned towards the hill; he had heard tell of the war-
"fare of Hygelac, the war-craft of the valiant; he trusted
"not in resistance, that he could defy the seamen, the
"travellers of the deep, could protect his treasure,
"his children, and his wife ; so he retired back there-
"from, the old king retired behind the earth-wall.
"Then was chase given to the Swedish Leeds ; the
" banners of Hygelac moved forward over that peaceful
"plain, and presently the Hrêthlings massed them- 2960
"selves upon the garrison. Then was Ongentheow,
"the gray-haired, driven to bay with sword-edges,
"insomuch that the mighty king was constrained to
"put up with the one-handed decision of Eofor. Him
"(Ongentheow) had Wulf son of Wonred fiercely
"attacked with weapon, so effectually, that with the
"stroke his blood flew from his veins out from under
"his hair. He was not daunted however, the aged
"Scilfing ; but he quickly repaid that deadly assault
"with worse barter, as soon as the mighty king 2970
"had collected himself. The brisk son of Wonred
"failed to give counter-blow to the old veteran, but
"he (Ongentheow) had first shorn the helmet on
"his head, so that blood-sprinkled he was forced to
"bow, he fell on the ground ;—he was not at that time
"death-doomed as yet, but he recovered from it, though
"the wound had touched him close. Then did Hygelac's
"valiant thane (i. e. Eofor) let his broad blade, gigant-
"esque old sword, his dwarf-wrought helmet, break 2980
"over the shield-wall ; then crouched the king, the

"people's shepherd, he was fatally smitten. Then were
"there many who bound up his brother's wounds (of
"Wulf the brother of Eofor), who quickly raised him
"up, when they had got the ground cleared, so that
"they had command of the place of battle. Meanwhile
"warrior stripped warrior; he (Eofor) captured on
"Ongentheow the iron breast-mail, his hard sword
"with hilt, and his helmet likewise, the grey-beard's
"accoutrements;—to Hygelac he bare them. He
"accepted the spoils, and made him a fair promise of
2990 "rewards before his Leeds, and he kept his word; he,
"the lord of the Goths, the son of Hrêthel, when he
"arrived at his mansion, repaid Jofor and Wulf for that
"war-brunt, with treasure extraordinary; he gave to
"each of them a hundred thousand of land and collars
"of filigree; none could jeer at them for those rewards,
"not a man in the world, since they had achieved those
"exploits;—and moreover he bestowed upon Jofor his
"only daughter, to make his home honourable, and for
"a pledge of loyalty.

"Such is the feud and the enmity and the deadly
3000 "grudge of the men, even the Swedish Leeds, who, as
"I apprehend, will attack us, as soon as they shall learn
"that our prince is dead, he who whilere hath upheld
"against hostilities, our treasure and our realm[1], was
"master of public counsel, or won ever-increasing
"glory in war. Now is quickness best, that we should
"there look upon the mighty king, and bring him who
3010 "gave us bracelets, on to the funeral-pile. It is not
"meet that some trifling matter be consumed with the
"high-souled man; but yonder is a hoard of precious

---

[1] Müllenhoff first pointed out that line 3005 must be omitted.

"things, gold uncounted, frightfully bargained for, and
"now at last jewels purchased with the hero's own
"life; those must fire devour, the flame must enfold
"them; never a warrior wear ornament for memorial,
"nor maiden sheen have on her neck the decorated
"collar, but on the contrary must in dejected mood
"and stripped of gold ornaments tread often and often
"the land of the stranger, now the army leader 3020
"hath laid aside laughter, game, and glee.   Therefore
"shall many a spear in the cold of the morning be
"clutched in men's grasp, hoisted in the hand; no
"swough of harp shall waken the warriors: but the
"bleak raven fluttering over carnage shall chatter
"abundantly, recount to the eagle of his luck at the
"spread, while alongside of the wolf he stripped the
"slain."

Thus was the ardent youth discoursing of painful
themes; he erred not widely of events or words.   All 3030
the troop arose, they went unjoyous, under the Eagle's
Crag, with gushing tears, to behold the tremendous
sight.   They found there, on the sand, bereft of life, and
keeping his helpless bed, the man who had given them
rings in times bygone; there had the final day come to
the valiant, in that the warlike king, the prince of the
Wederas, had perished with a death heroic.

. . . never saw they frightfuller object—the dragon
on the ground there right before their face, the loath- 3040
some beast lying dead; all scorched with flames was the
fire-drake, the grisly gruesome pest; it was fifty foot-
measurements long where it lay; in the pride of the air
he had been supreme during the hours of night, and then
down would he return back again to reconnoitre his

lair:—now he was there stock dead, had made his last use of earthly caverns. By the side of it stood pots and bowls; there dishes lay about, and swords of price, rusty and corroded, as if they in earth's lap a
3050 thousand winters there had sojourned; forasmuch as that patrimony, huge and vast, that gold of ancient men, had been closed about with enchantment; and therefore that treasure-chamber might not be touched by any one of mankind, save in so far as God himself, the true king of achievements, should grant to the man of his choice to open the hoard the sorcerers' hold:—even to such one of mankind whomso he deemed to be meet.

XLII.

Reflections upon the great event. Wiglaf publishes Beowulf's dying orders. Preparations for the bale-fire. The cavern is rifled, and the treasures are piled on a wagon to follow the bier. The last of the Dragon.

Then was it manifest, that good luck attended not upon the course of them who by unlawful means had
3060 closely safe-guarded valuables under the mound. At first the keeper slew one here and there; at length the feud had grown to be expiated furiously. By a heroic death therefore in some manner should a brave warrior accomplish the end of life's record, seeing that he cannot much longer as a man in the midst of his kins-folk inhabit the mead-hall. Such was Beowulf's lot, when he went forth to seek the Keeper of the barrow, went to seek deadly strife, he himself knew not by what means his severance from the world was destined
3070 to happen, according as the mighty captains, when they that deposited there, had uttered a deep spell to

hold till doomsday, that the man who invaded that ground should be criminally guilty, cabined in heathen fanes, fast bound with hell-bands, penally doomed; yet never did he at any previous time more effectually experience the gold-bestowing favour of God.

Wiglâf son of Wihstan lifted up his voice: "Often "must many a brave man, by the will of one, endure "tribulation, as it hath happened to us. We were not "able to convince our beloved master, the shepherd of 3080 "the kingdom, by any reasoning, that he should not "challenge yon gold-warden, but should leave him to "lie where he had long been, and to dwell in his haunts "till the end of the world, fulfil high destiny. The "hoard is laid open to our view, fearfully purchased; "too overpowering was that boon which attracted our "prince thither. I was in the interior of the place, and "I explored the whole of it, the stores of the chamber, "inasmuch as the way had been opened for me and "that by no gentle means, passage was permitted in 3090 "under the earthen dome. Hurriedly I grappled with "my hands a huge mighty burden of hoarded treasures; "out hither I bore them to the feet of my king. He "was still alive then, wise and sensible; freely did he "talk, the aged one in death-pang; and he commanded "me to give you his greeting, he bade that you should "construct, in memory of your chieftain's deeds, upon "the scene of the bale-fire, a barrow of the highest, "mighty and magnifical, according as he was of all men "the warrior most famous, through the wide earth, so 3100 "long as he might enjoy the wealth of his castle.

"Go to, let us now hasten, a second time, to see and to "visit the ruck of jewels, the spectacle beneath the earth-

"work.   I will be your guide, so that ye shall have your
"fill of seeing close at hand, collars and bullion gold.

 " Let the bier be ready, promptly equipped, attending
"us as we go forth of this place, and so let us convey
"our master, the beloved man, to the place where he
"shall tarry long in the safe keeping of the Almighty."

3110   Then did the son of Wihstan order his brave warriors
that they should issue commands to many homestead-
owners, for them to haul pyre-timber from far to meet
the occasion of the Ruler of men :—" Now must fire
"devour, the scowling flame must wash, the Pillar of
"warriors, him who often stood the shock of the iron
"shower, what time the storm of missiles, urged by
"bow-strings, hurtled over the shield-wall, the shaft
"did its duty, with feather-fittings eager it backed up the
"arrow's point."

3120   Thereupon the prudent son of Wihstan called out of
the squadron some thanes of the king, seven of them together, the choicest ; he made the eighth, and went with
them under the dangerous roof; a warrior bore in hand a
flaming torch, and he walked in front.   It was not staked
upon lot who should have the looting of that hoard, when
the warriors had partly taken a view of it in its keeper-
less state occupying the chamber, lying helpless.   Little
3130 did any man scruple that they should with all dispatch
convey abroad the valuable treasures; the Dragon
moreover they haled, they shoved the Worm over the
precipitous cliff, they let the wave take him, the flood
engulf him, that warder of precious spoils.

 There was coiled gold laden upon wagon, countless
in quantity of every kind ;—the Etheling was borne on
a bier, the hoary warrior, to Hrónesness.

XLIII.

The Funeral and the Epitaph.

For him then did the Leeds of the Goths construct a pyre upon the earth, one of no mean dimensions, hung about with helmets, with battle-boards, with bright 3140 byrnies, as he had requested; then did they, heaving deep sighs, lay in the midst of it the illustrious chieftain, the hero, the beloved lord. Then began the warriors to kindle upon the hill the hugest of bale-fires; the wood-smoke mounted up black over the combustive mass, the roaring blaze shot aloft, mingled with the howling of the wind-currents; until the swelter-ing element had demolished the bone-house. With hearts distressed and care-laden minds they mourned their liege lord's death; likewise a dirge of sorrow 3150 [1] *was sung in honour of Beowulf by the aged dame, her hair bound up, her soul sorrowing; she said repeatedly, that she sorely dreaded for herself evil days, much blood-shed, the warrior's horror, shame and captivity.* Heaven swallowed the smoke.

Then did the people of the Wederas construct a tumulus on the hill; it was high and broad, to sea-voyagers widely conspicuous; and during ten days 3160 they laboured about the building of the war-hero's beacon: they surrounded the ashes of the conflagration with an embankment in such wise as men of eminent skill could contrive it with noblest effect. They de-posited in the barrow collars and brilliants, the whole

[1] Here are six mutilated lines, in which the most leading word means 'woman,' and, with Grein's emendation, 'old woman.' This seems to have suggested Hecuba to Professor Bugge, and with his talent at re-construction he has stopped the gap as in the Italics above.

of such trappings as war-breathing men had recently captured in the Hoard; they abandoned the accumulated wealth of eorlas for the earth to retain it, gold in marl, where it now still continues to be as useless to mankind as it was erst.

3170   Then there rode around the tumulus war-chiefs, sons of ethelings, twelve in all; they would bewail their loss, bemoan the king, recite an elegy, and celebrate his name.   They admired his manhood, and they loftily appraised his daring work ; as it is fitting that a man should with words extol his liege lord, should cherish him in his affections, when h e must take his departure from the tenemental body.

Thus did the Leeds of the Goths, the companions of 3180 his hearth, lament the fall of their lord ;—they said that he was of all kings i n the world, the mildest and most affable to his men; most genial to his Leeds; and most desirous of PRAISE.